ROSS

7 Brides for 7 Blackthornes (Book 3)

LYNN RAYE HARRIS

H.O.T. Publishing, LLC

The Hostile Operations Team® and Lynn Raye Harris® are
trademarks of H.O.T. Publishing, LLC.

Printed in the United States of America

First Printing, 2019

For rights inquires, visit www.LynnRayeHarris.com

Ross
Copyright © 2019 by Lynn Raye Harris
Cover Design Copyright © 2019 Damonza

ISBN: 978-1-941002-49-0

7 Brides for 7 Blackthornes

Meet the Blackthorne men, each one as hot, fast, and smooth as the whisky that built the family fortune, and the yachts and race cars that bear their name. From proud Scottish stock, Blackthornes never lose. But, one by one, the seven sexy men in this family are about to risk everything when they fall for strong and beautiful women who test their mettle in life, and love.

Devlin (#1) - Barbara Freethy
Jason (#2) - Julia London
Ross (#3) - Lynn Raye Harris
Phillip (#4) - Cristin Harber
Brock (#5) - Roxanne St. Claire
Logan (#6) - Samantha Chase
Trey (#7) - Christie Ridgway

Chapter 1

"The Blackthorne Whisky car takes the lead! Ross Blackthorne is really making a run for the Cup this year and this race might just be the proof he's got what it takes—oh no, he's on fire! Something just exploded in there—and Blackthorne is spinning out of control as he gets clipped from behind! His spotter's telling him to get out of there quick! But he's got to bring the car to a stop before he can do that. Oh wow, this is a messy one, look at those cars pile up. And Ross Blackthorne needs to get out of that blaze before it gets any worse. Holy heck, now he's airborne…"

"I'M FINE," Ross said, pushing away the nurse's soft, prying hands. He could still smell burning rubber and oil. He'd be a bit stiff tomorrow, maybe a few bruises, but otherwise he'd be fine. Not that he'd expected anything less. The cars were built with plenty of protective systems and racing was far safer than it used to be.

Drivers walked away from crashes that would have killed them previously. There hadn't been a driver fatality on the track in almost twenty years. He was glad he hadn't changed that statistic tonight.

Martin Temple stood with hands on hips and stared at Ross. Temple was gray-haired and wiry, and the way he stared reminded Ross—uncomfortably—of his father. Lately, Dad had been pressuring him to head over to the Blackthorne Distillery near Lexington, Kentucky, and put in some time learning about the bourbon business. But Ross was busy with the racing team, which was headquartered near Louisville for the time being, and hadn't managed it yet. He didn't want to manage it.

The nurse slipped out the door. Silence stretched until Ross broke it.

"We were winning," Ross said. He was still pissed about losing his shot at victory today. It'd taken a lot of fancy talking to get his father to agree to sponsoring a racing team, and now this. Just when he'd been on the cusp of proving that the expense was worth it in terms of advertising and brand recognition, he'd blown an engine on the final lap.

And he'd done it on national television in full view of his family—*if* they'd been watching. He hoped like hell they had not. Especially his dad.

Blowing an engine was one thing. But spinning out of control and flying through the air while on fire was quite another. Landing upside down was simply a bonus, especially when you had to climb through roaring flames to get out of the cage.

These days, Ross didn't think it would take much to convince Graham Blackthorne that it was time his son hung up the racing suit and put on a business suit. He'd been hinting at it a lot lately. If he'd been watching, the accident might be just the excuse he needed.

"Yep," Martin replied. "But that's racing for you. One little thing goes wrong, and it all goes wrong."

"What the hell did you do to my engine, Martin?"

Martin frowned. "Now don't you start that crap with me, Ross Blackthorne. You were pushing the car hard. It happens. Engines blow under that kind of stress. The rest of it was bad luck based on your position."

Ross shoved a hand through his hair. Engine failures were definitely a part of life in racing. He knew it as well as anyone. But dammit, why'd it have to happen on the last lap when the win was within reach? When he'd been about to prove to his father that the millions of dollars poured into the racing team was money well spent? Jack Daniel and Jim Beam had pulled out of sponsoring stock cars lately. Ross didn't want Blackthorne to follow suit.

His brother Devlin had the yachts. Ross wanted cars. The difference was that Dad was also a sailor and he understood yachts. He didn't understand cars. Didn't much care. Ross had a steeper mountain to climb—and the climb had just gotten harder if his dad saw that race.

"Yeah, yeah. Engines fail. It would've been nice if it could have waited another lap though."

Martin looked troubled. "I know, kid. I'm sorry."

"So we'll win the next one. Nothing we can do about this one."

"That's right. We'll win the next one," Martin said. But he didn't sound like he believed it.

Ross stood up, suddenly weary. He was still wearing his fire suit with the Blackthorne logo emblazoned on the front and he wanted to get out of it. Then he wanted to take a shower and think about how to spin this loss to his father.

Before he took the first step, his phone rang. He picked it up, wondering when he'd gotten it from his assistant. He didn't carry it while racing. But here it was and that meant someone had put it near him at some point during the past twenty minutes.

He looked at the screen—and instantly wished he hadn't. He debated sending the call to voicemail. But if his father had seen the crash, he'd probably be worried. It wasn't fair to refuse to answer under those circumstances.

Ross slid the bar. "Hey, Dad."

"Are you okay, son?"

"Yes, sir. I'm fine."

He thought he heard his dad swear beneath his breath. "Good. Because that looked like a hell of a mess."

Great.

"The engine blew. It happens."

"You could have been killed," Dad said. "Your mother would never forgive me if—"

He broke off and Ross's throat tightened. Yeah, bring Mom into it. He needed to call her later. She was in Paris and it was late there, so she probably didn't know. He also didn't think American stock car races were broadcast on French television. He had time.

"I know it looked bad, but the cars are safe. The systems are designed to do what they did. I'm not hurt." Mostly.

"It's risky. Too risky."

Ross had the sensation of a noose closing around his neck. "Can we talk later, Dad? I'd like to get out of this suit and into some street clothes—"

"No," Graham said, cutting him off. "We're going to talk now."

Ross gritted his teeth. He had a lot of adrenaline flowing through his system and he wanted to punch something. But there was nothing to punch. Except a wall. Or Martin. He felt like Martin might punch back though. "Yes, sir."

"I'm thankful you're alive. Incredibly thankful. But this seals it for me. You've been entirely too reckless with your life, Ross. It's time you did something safer."

Ross froze. *He'd* been reckless? Dad still hadn't admitted that Mom had left him, or why. How reckless had he been to lose Mom? And how prideful not to apologize for whatever he'd done and beg her to come back? No Blackthorne had ever gotten divorced in the history of Blackthornes. Were his parents about to be the first? What happened to the brand then?

His cousin Brock was probably having a coronary considering it.

Focus. "Listen Dad—"

"No. Everything we are as Blackthornes, our history, our destiny—we owe it to the whisky. It's our heritage, our pride, and it's time you took more than a passing interest in just precisely what it is that keeps this family in the position we enjoy. You need to do your part, Ross."

Ross's blood was turning to ice. Fury rolled inside him. He wanted to ask about Mom, but he sensed that wouldn't go over so well.

And do his part? He'd been doing his part as an ambassador for the brand. Ross Blackthorne the racing driver couldn't go out on the street without being recognized in most places. He smiled and signed autographs and answered questions, because he was a damned brand ambassador who cared about his family legacy. Just like his brothers and cousins.

"But Devlin—" he began.

"Devlin," his father said, cutting him off, "is building and selling sailboats in addition to racing them. Can you tell me how running cars on the NASCAR circuit is going to make the family money? Are you going to be selling stock cars, Ross?"

"No, but—"

"No, of course not. You can't build and sell stock cars to the luxury market, which is something your brother can do with boats. Devlin has proven himself. But you, Ross…" His father sighed. A disappointed sound that filled Ross with a mixture of fury and sadness at the same time. As the third son, he'd always felt like a spare child. He didn't doubt his parents loved him, but he'd never felt like they had specific expectations for him either. "I've indulged you too much. You're reporting to the Blackthorne Distillery for work."

Ross swallowed his fury. Dad was just mad—and more than a little lost without Mom—but he'd get over it. And Mom would come home again.

"I can't stop driving or I won't have a shot at the Cup this year."

And this year he had a chance to win it. A damned good one. He was driving better than ever. The leader board could change several times by the end, but he'd won two races already and finished in the top five six times. The rest were top ten finishes. Surely Dad wouldn't jeopardize the opportunity with this idea of Ross working at the distillery. It would be good for the brand if Ross won the Cup. If he did, he'd been thinking about going out on his own—not that he'd told anyone that.

Ross Blackthorne Motorsports instead of Blackthorne Racing. He'd have more freedom to do what he wanted, to expand the team and bring on younger drivers to train.

He'd also be able to open the performance division he'd wanted to start—and build a garage where he could help people who needed basic transportation to afford reliable used cars.

But now Dad was throwing everything into chaos. All because of a race that Ross had nearly won. Nearly, but not quite. The finish line had been within reach—just like the finish line to creating his own motorsport brand.

Crash, burn, done.

"I've given the order to Martin. You're finished racing, Ross. Report to the distillery in two days."

"I need more time than that," Ross growled. "We aren't *in* Kentucky right now. I've got to get back there and—"

"One week. No more."

The phone went dead. Ross turned to look at Martin. But Martin was already gone.

———

HOLLY BROOKS SAT at her desk in the Blackthorne Distillery's office building and flicked through the tabs on her browser. She had a meeting with the master distiller in twenty minutes to go over plans for a new line of flavored bourbons—ginger, vanilla, and cherry to complement the honey and cinnamon they already sold—and she was doing last minute research on their competitors' offerings.

She opened a new window to type in another competitor's name when a headline caught her attention.

ROSS BLACKTHORNE IN FIERY CRASH

Holly bit her lip as she clicked the link. There was a picture of a burning car lying upside down. And then there was a picture of Ross Blackthorne in his black and gold racing suit, helmet cradled in his right arm, frowning as the emergency crew directed fire retardant at the car.

Holly shivered. She knew what fire could do to end dreams.

Ross was alive and apparently uninjured. She didn't really know him, though he'd toured the distillery once. Precisely once, about three months ago. They'd been introduced. She remembered the exact moment as if it were embedded beneath her skin for all time. She'd been testing the mash and she'd been sweating in the heat of the fermentation house, a bandanna tied over her hair, no makeup, and baggy overalls. She'd heard the door open and then Uncle Evan was there with the most strikingly handsome man she'd ever seen in her life.

Ross Blackthorne was tall, lean, with dark, slightly curly hair and brown eyes. His face had seemed carved from marble it was so pretty, with sharp cheekbones and a perfect nose. He was tanned and handsome, and he'd looked right through her as he'd shaken her hand politely. She'd stammered and blushed but he hadn't noticed before Uncle Evan whisked him away.

Thank God.

Holly growled. Why was she clicking on articles about him anyway? He'd been polite enough, but she knew a rich playboy when she saw one. Spoiled, privileged, and filled with too much testosterone that made him do stupid things like drive flaming racecars.

She told herself to close the tab, but of course she didn't. She read the article. Then she clicked over to a related article that showed Ross in a bar, surrounded by smiling women. His mouth was open as he laughed, straight white teeth flashing in his perfectly handsome face. The article was from last week, so not an accurate representation of how he'd spent the night after the crash. Still, she imagined he spent most nights that way. He was too gorgeous and too rich not to.

And those women were beautiful, too. Tight clothes, curvy figures, long flowing hair. Perfect makeup. They looked like movie stars to her. Nothing like a girl in a bandanna and overalls with her hands—sans manicure and polish—dipping into a lake of fragrant corn mash.

There was a knock on her door. She minimized the browser as the door opened to reveal Uncle Evan. "Morning, Holly," he said as he came inside.

"Morning, Uncle Evan. I was just doing some research before our meeting."

Uncle Evan had been the master distiller for the past three years—ever since their family distillery had been bought out by the Blackthornes. It was a job she wanted someday, but she still had a lot to learn. She'd wanted to be the master distiller for Brooks Creek, but that brand was gone now. She felt the same pang she always did when she thought of her family label and how quickly everything changed. They might have made it if not for the fire that wiped out their three main barrelhouses and all their best whisky.

"Good, good," Uncle Evan said. "I'm sure you're going to dazzle me with your plans."

"I hope so." And then she hoped he managed to dazzle the Blackthornes with her suggestion. Nothing would get done without the head office's say so.

"I wanted to talk to you about something," he said, shutting the door behind him. "Before we meet with the team."

"Okay." Holly nervously picked up her notebook. The spirit-making team was another name for the production staff, which these days included a lot more people than it had in the days of Brooks Creek. But that's what happened when a major distiller bought your product and recipes and incorporated them into their own brand. The Blackthornes made some of the finest whisky Holly had ever tasted—but it wasn't technically bourbon, though it was bourbon-style whisky.

Buying the old Brooks Creek distillery and expanding it right here in Bourbon County was what made Blackthorne an official bourbon maker. It was a market they were primed to dominate.

"We've had a lot of autonomy," Uncle Evan said. "Graham Blackthorne is a shrewd businessman and a fine whisky maker."

"Why do I sense a *but?*" Holly asked when he didn't continue.

"Because I'm about to tell you something you don't want to hear."

Holly's belly twisted. "What now? We're being thrown out? The Blackthornes are sending their own people to take over?"

Uncle Evan's eyes widened. "Holly, we *are* their people. We've been here since they bought our stock and our equipment, and we've helped expand production. The Blackthornes have been good to us."

Holly felt herself reddening. They had, but she still hated that one fire had brought them to this. That she would never make her family whisky under their own name again. All thanks to her idiot brother and his arrogance.

That's not fair, Holly.

He couldn't have foreseen a lightning strike and high winds. Except he could have if he'd listened to her advice.

Not that she was bitter.

"So what is it then?" she asked.

Uncle Evan came and sat down in one of the armchairs crammed into her little office. She could have had a bigger one, but she hadn't wanted it. She hadn't wanted anyone to think she wasn't working her way to the top on her own merit.

Being the master distiller's niece was a fine line to walk when you wanted to earn the job for yourself someday. People talked, but they weren't going to talk about Holly

Brooks not doing what she was paid to do or getting special privileges.

He folded his hands over his belly. One of the changes when the Blackthornes took over was how Uncle Evan often dressed. She missed his overalls and plaid shirts, though he still wore them sometimes.

But he mostly wore shirts and ties and had meetings with people to promote the Blackthorne whisky they made here (which did not include Blackthorne Gold, the most exclusive whisky the Blackthornes made)—though she was the one who often developed his talking points.

In the beginning, she'd attended a lot of the meetings with him. But these days he was comfortable going alone.

"We're getting a Blackthorne on staff," he began, and her heart plummeted. "Graham is sending one of his sons to learn the business."

Holly felt lightheaded for a second. It wasn't easy being a woman in this business, especially a woman who wanted to run the distillery someday. Technically, she already ran the distillery, but Uncle Evan was the one in charge.

But with a Blackthorne here she would never get the job.

But did it really matter who held the master distiller title? Uncle Evan might be the one with the most knowledge about the whisky and the distilling process, but she was his right hand—and she kept the day-to-day operations running smoothly for him.

If she'd been the one running operations instead of her brother Ricky a few years ago, maybe they wouldn't have lost the barrel houses. If Uncle Evan and Dad had been interested in more than making the whisky back then, maybe things would have been different.

"Okay," she said, resolving to stay cool and pushing down all the family drama and bitterness that still upset her. "Which Blackthorne is gracing us with his presence? And when may we expect him?"

Uncle Evan gave her a grin. "Ross Blackthorne will be here next week."

Holly blinked. "Ross? But he's a racecar driver! And the worst kind of spoiled rich guy possible. There's no way he's serious about this. Have you seen him spraying champagne on scantily clad women after he wins a race?"

Uncle Evan arched an eyebrow. "Been checking up on Ross Blackthorne, Hollykins?"

Holly blushed. She ducked her head to hide it, but she didn't think Uncle Evan was fooled. "No, but he was in the news this morning and I saw some photos. He flipped his car on the track this weekend. Caught it on fire. Is he in any shape to come to work?"

She knew he hadn't been injured but he must at least be sore. Maybe even shook up.

Uncle Evan sighed. "Walked away without a scratch, I hear. Bruised a bit maybe. I do believe there was an ultimatum issued. I take it Graham Blackthorne wasn't too pleased with that wreck. We're getting Ross and we've got to teach him a thing or two about the business. Maybe if we do that well, he'll fall in love with the process. Or maybe he'll quit and go back to his cars. Either way, we're getting a Blackthorne—and like it or not, we've got to work with him."

"Assign him to bottling or something. That will keep him busy."

He was such an expert with opening bottles and spraying champagne on people that it was only fitting he put some alcohol *into* the bottle for a change. But she didn't say it.

"Sorry, Hols, can't do that. Ross is the son of the owner. He's coming here as an executive vice president, which means he's getting fast-tracked—and you're going to teach him what he needs to know."

Holly screeched as she shot from her chair. "Me? Why me? I've got work to do. He'll only get in the way—besides, I've got too much on my plate already. He'll slow me down."

Executive vice president her butt. That's what all these rich people did. Gave themselves lofty titles and didn't care about the work. Well, she didn't want any part of it.

"Holly Margaret Brooks," her uncle said sternly as he stood again. "Graham Blackthorne asked for my best man to train his son. I told him my best man was a woman —*you*. I won't lie to the man and give him anyone else. He asked for the best. He's getting it."

Holly felt a mixture of pride and exasperation. And love, because she loved Uncle Evan. He was all she had left of her father. Dad had a heart attack right after they lost their warehouses full of whisky and never recovered. Uncle Evan had been her rock through everything that followed. Still was. How could she refuse him?

"Argh," she said "Not fair."

"You're as good as your dad was, Holly. You'll be better than both of us when it's your turn at the helm. This is your chance to win over a Blackthorne—hell, to impress them all by the time you're done. Don't mess it up."

Holly didn't feel nearly as optimistic as Uncle Evan did. But she knew when she was caught. Ross Blackthorne wasn't going to give two shits about the operations, but what could she do? "I'll do my best with him," she said tightly.

Uncle Evan grinned. "I know you will. It's why I chose you."

"Thanks a lot."

"Cheer up, girly. You've got this."

Holly slumped down in her chair after he left and pulled up her browser again. She had a little more research to do on their competitors before the new product meeting.

But the first thing that popped onto her screen was that smiling photo of Ross Blackthorne. Handsome, cocky, too appealing for his own good. He knew he was special. His look said it all. His hair was just a little shaggy, and he had a sexy scruff of a beard. He was rugged, masculine. He made women melt. They were melting all around him in that photo, their limbs positively droopy as they leaned toward him.

Holly straightened. Well, she wasn't melting. And she wasn't going to smile vacuously at him like that either. No way was she falling at his golden-boy feet and letting him walk all over her, no matter how pretty he was.

No siree, Ross Blackthorne wasn't getting an easy pass from her. If he wanted to learn the whisky business, he was going to have to work for it.

Chapter 2

Ross got up far earlier than he liked, dressed in dark jeans and a button-down shirt, and climbed into his red LaFerrari Aperta. Maybe he should have put on a suit and tie, but screw it. He wasn't hanging out any longer than he had to. A few days at most.

He hoped.

He gunned the car onto the highway, swinging around the ramp at speed, heading for the Blackthorne Distillery located about an hour away in a little town outside Lexington.

It was a lovely, sunny Thursday morning. He could have waited until Monday, but he'd decided that the sooner he started, the sooner he could get this over with and get back to racing.

Horses grazed in herds behind white split rail fencing, their coats shiny in the morning sun. The bluegrass sparkled with dew and Ross had to slide on a pair of Oakleys to protect his eyes as he drove east.

The drive went by quickly, not only because he was in

an exotic sports car that boogied, but also because the countryside was pretty and his mind wandered as he drove.

He liked it here. It wasn't Maine, especially the family estate at King Harbor with its sweeping views of the water, but Kentucky had its charms. He liked the South, and he liked Southern accents. Particularly when they whispered in his ear while he lost himself in the arms of the pretty women to whom they belonged.

Right now, he was glad to be far away from King Harbor. If he had to face his father, he'd probably snap. He'd called Devlin last night. His brother was too cheery for words these days. Came from settling down with Hannah Reid, he guessed.

"Any advice, Dev?" he'd asked his brother.

"Honestly? Just do it, Ross. Make an effort, do your best, fail as badly as you're going to, then go back to your cars."

Ross had been a little taken aback that Devlin assumed he'd fail so easily. It wasn't that Ross didn't understand the whisky, or appreciate it. It just wasn't his calling. The power that came from a finely tuned engine and stiff suspension—that was his jam. But here he was, driving toward the distillery and uncertain how he'd ever escape it.

"What if Dad doesn't approve?" he'd asked.

Devlin had sighed. "Dad's distracted and twitchy right now. He'll relax when Mom comes back."

"Is she still in Paris?"

"So far as I know."

"You haven't talked to her?"

"Not lately. You?"

"No. She sent a text about the accident and we texted back and forth for a few minutes. But when I asked when she was coming home, she didn't reply. I haven't tried since."

"Yeah," Devlin said sadly. "I don't know what's going on with them exactly, but I wish Dad would go get her."

"Do you really think that would work?"

"No, probably not."

They'd talked a little while longer, then Ross hung up and fell into bed for a few hours before getting up early to start the trek to the distillery. He was no more settled about it this morning than he had been when Dad issued the ultimatum. Martin assured him everything would be fine with the racing team. The car would be ready to go for the next race, no problem.

Except Ross wouldn't be driving. It would be Eric Vicker, a young driver who'd been recruited to the team a few months ago. Eric was good, but it sure was going to hurt to watch him drive the races that Ross should be in.

After nearly an hour on the road, Ross turned the LaFerrari onto the short drive that led to the distillery. It was a picturesque setting, with mature trees, a creek that flowed lazily past the main building, and rolling fields dotted with horses and sheep. There was an old Victorian farmhouse sitting on a hill overlooking the distillery. It had once belonged to the Brooks family from whom they'd bought the property a few years ago. No one lived in it now, though.

Ross pulled into the main parking lot and shut off the engine. A group of people who'd been crossing the parking lot stopped to stare. He got out of the car and locked it up, tipping his chin to the crowd. Maybe he should have parked in the back instead of out here with the tourists. He gazed up at the buildings, taking in the gray and white wooden facades with their black shutters and red doors. The Blackthorne thistle and barrel label was prominent on the main building. Pride swelled within. He'd grown up with that label, grown up with everything it had given him.

It was more than a label, though. It was family and tradition and hard work and heritage. He was a Blackthorne, and he cared about that very much—even if he didn't personally want to learn the whisky business. A door opened off to his left. He turned to see a woman with long red hair striding toward him, holding a clipboard. She was frowning. He took a moment to appreciate the picture she made.

Flowing hair, flashing blue eyes, a full mouth. She was wearing a white shirt with buttons, black leggings, and a pair of white Converse. She looked casual and pretty—and irritated, he noted with some confusion. He glanced behind him. There was no one—well, tourists, but they were making their way to the main entrance now. A little boy and his dad lingered, taking pictures of the car.

"You want to sit in it?" Ross asked.

The boy's eyes grew wide. He looked up at his dad. "Could I?"

"I don't know, Timmy…"

Ross unlocked the car and opened the door. "It's okay. Take his picture in the driver's seat."

The woman had stopped, hugging her clipboard to her chest. When his eyes met hers, she started forward again. Slowly this time. The man and his son came over and the little boy got into the car.

"This car," the man began. "The cost. Are you sure you want him in there?"

Ross laughed. "Sure. You can go next if you like. I'll take your picture."

"Man," the guy said. "I really would." He cocked his head as he stared at Ross. "You're Ross Blackthorne."

"Guilty," Ross said with a grin.

"That was some wreck you had. Glad you're okay."

"Thanks. It happens."

"I was pulling for you. Blackthorne is my favorite whisky. I really thought you had it."

"I thought so too. Next time."

"Yeah, next time."

Ross spent the next few minutes showing off the car, taking pictures, and chatting with the man and his son. He was aware of the woman behind him the entire time. It was almost as if he could feel her stare in his bones. And it wasn't a friendly stare.

When the man and boy were finished and heading toward the visitor entrance, Ross clicked the car locked again and turned. She was still standing there. She didn't smile.

"Hi, Mr. Blackthorne. I'm Holly Brooks. I'm here to show you around."

"Hi, Holly," he said, holding out his hand. "You can call me Ross."

She hesitated but then she thrust her hand out. He grasped it, palm to palm. The sizzle that skipped through his nerve endings was a bit of a surprise. She seemed surprised too because she yanked her hand away and wrapped it around her clipboard.

"Welcome to your distillery, mister, er, Ross."

"You said your name is Brooks?"

"Yes."

"Your family owned this place before mine did. I understand that Brooks Creek bourbon was some of the best around."

"It is. We still make it. Under your label now. Blackthorne's Brooks Creek Select."

She seemed annoyed that he didn't know it already. He wasn't used to women being annoyed with him. "I'll remember that. Did you work at the Brooks Creek distillery?"

"I did. I'm a distiller, same as my daddy before me. Same as my uncle now."

Ross offered her a smile. His smiles usually disarmed women. She didn't appear very disarmed. "I descend from distillers," he said, "but I'm not one. Apparently, my father intends for me to learn."

"You grew up in the Blackthorne family. Surely you know something about the process."

"Something, yes. But I never intended to go into the family business."

Her gaze slipped beyond him to the car for a second. Then her eyes fixed on his again. "That's a nice car you have."

Her tone said that she expected the car cost approximately the GDP of a small country and that she also thought he was compensating for something. He almost laughed. Holly Brooks knew how to throw shade.

"Thank you," he said.

"It was nice of you to let that little boy and his dad sit in it."

"When I was a kid, I loved cars. Made my day when one of my dad's friends let me sit in a rare Corvette he'd bought. I think I was about four. I never forgot it."

She cleared her throat. "Yes, well, I came to tell you that you should move it to the employee area. We've cleared a spot for you. I don't think anyone expected you to show up in an exotic, though maybe we should have. But nobody will scrape your paint and the car will probably be safer back there than out here in the public lot."

Ross studied her. Her body language was more than dismissive. It was downright hostile. He clicked the doors open. "Why don't you get in and show me where this spot is, Holly?"

She opened her mouth to argue, he was sure, but then she snapped it closed and started for the passenger side of the car. "Fine. Let's go."

———

THE LAST THING Holly wanted to do was climb into a confined space with Ross Blackthorne, but Uncle Evan had warned her to be accommodating to their guest—so she was going to be accommodating. Besides, it would be easier to ride around the side of the building with him than to tell him where to go and then wait for him to find his way to the correct entrance.

She was still thinking about the look on that little boy's face as Ross let him climb around inside the car when the man himself settled in beside her and the engine growled to life. Holly stared straight ahead, at the black dashboard with its red detailing, and felt the seat hugging her in place. It was definitely a gorgeous car. A very expensive car. And he'd let a kid inside it.

She scowled. Didn't make him a saint or anything. He was nice to a little kid, but he was still a daredevil and a womanizer who probably didn't want to be here. Which meant he wasn't planning to take the distillery seriously. She'd had enough of that with her brother.

"Seat belt," Ross said.

They were only going around the building but she snapped it into place anyway. He put the car in gear and backed up. Then he gunned it and the vehicle shot forward like a racehorse leaping out of the gate. Holly may have squeaked.

"Turn there," she said, pointing.

But Ross kept going, swinging the car onto the main road and accelerating toward town.

"You missed the turn," she said stupidly. She could smell him in this confined space, or maybe that was just the expensive leather of the seats.

"Why don't you give me a tour of the town and show me where the barrelhouses are?"

"I…" She swallowed. This was *not* what she'd expected to be doing right now. She was supposed to bring Ross up to the conference room where he could meet the distillers and office staff. But apparently that's not what he wanted, so that's not what they were doing. "Fine, if that's what you want."

"I do." He pointed at a massive gray building with the Blackthorne logo painted on the front. "Barrel house?"

"Yes. We have ten of them now, since your father bought our operation. We had three originally."

"And you lost them in a fire, right?"

"With about forty-two thousand barrels of whisky. Yes." The barrelhouses had been too close together and the fire spread quickly. She'd long argued for moving the stock, separating it, but her brother had argued that they didn't have the money to build new warehouses. The more they produced, however, the more worried she'd gotten. But since he'd gotten a dual degree in chemistry and business—and since he was a man—her father and uncle had listened to him instead of her.

"Next season, Holly," he'd said. "We'll have the money then."

Next season never came because the fire destroyed nearly all their stock. And their finances along with it. The offer from Blackthorne Enterprises was the only thing that saved them. Except it didn't save them completely. It consumed them and brought them under the Blackthorne label.

Which is how she found herself in a rare sports car with a handsome playboy who did what he wanted and to hell with everyone else. Anger flared deep inside. "People are waiting for you in the conference room. They've literally stopped what they're doing to welcome you to the distillery and you're making them wait while you go on a sightseeing tour."

He glanced at her, dark eyes widening slightly. With anger or surprise? She didn't know and she didn't care. Uncle Evan told her to be nice to the Blackthorne and she was blowing it.

But he deserved it. Inconsiderate jerk.

"You could have said so before," he told her, and guilt pricked to life inside her.

He was right. She could have. "You surprised me."

It wasn't much of an excuse, but it was the only one she had.

"So we'll head back. You can show me the barrel houses later." He pulled into the parking lot and carefully made a U-turn before driving back to the distillery. He followed her directions for where to park, then shut the car off and gripped the wheel with long fingers. "I don't think you like me," he said into the silence.

She started to deny it. But it was true, so why lie? Except now she felt even guiltier. Liking him wasn't a requirement, but she didn't have to be so obvious about it.

"I don't know you," she said truthfully.

"No, you don't. But you don't like me."

"I didn't say that."

"You didn't really have to."

"I'm sorry if I've given you that impression, Mr. Blackthorne. It's my job to welcome you, not make you uncomfortable."

"I'm not uncomfortable. Just surprised, I guess. Most people seem to like me well enough when we meet. But I think I may have made *you* uncomfortable."

Holly frowned. "Not at all."

"I shouldn't have ignored your instructions. Forgive me."

She swallowed. She certainly hadn't expected an apology. "We're here now. It's fine."

"I feel like there's something you aren't telling me."

Holly turned to him, surprised. He was studying her with those smoky brown eyes. She could understand why women melted. Not that she was in danger of it, but she got why. Even if she did, he wasn't likely to notice. She wasn't a Barbie doll with a perfect body that turned heads. She was just herself.

"The only thing I haven't told you is that we've met before. You don't seem to remember it."

It was his turn to look surprised. "That's because I don't. When was it?"

"When you toured the distillery three months ago. I was in the fermentation area, checking the mash. Uncle Evan took you through."

She saw the moment recognition dawned. "The girl in the overalls."

"That's right." She supposed it was something that he knew that much.

His gaze slipped over her face, down to her mouth, back up to her eyes. She hated the way her insides twisted.

"I'm sorry," he said. "But you don't look the same as you did that day. Your hair was covered. I'm sure I'd have recognized you today by the color alone had it not been."

"It's okay. I'm sure you meet so many women that they all run together in your head," she told him with a smile.

His eyes widened. Then he laughed. It was a rich sound. A sound that crawled inside her and made her belly warm.

"Maybe they do," he finally said. "But I have a feeling I'm not about to forget meeting you this time, Holly Brooks."

Chapter 3

Ross followed Holly into the stillhouse, watching her hips swing the entire way. She was pretty and prickly and he didn't know why that attracted him—but it did. He remembered the girl testing the mash that day. She'd had pretty eyes, a smattering of light freckles on her face, but her hair had been hidden beneath a blue bandanna. He'd said he would have recognized her by her hair color today, but the truth was he should have recognized her by her eyes.

He just hadn't. Probably because he'd been here under protest that day as well. His father had been making noises about him joining the company, but Ross had been determined not to. He'd come to tour the facility in order to humor everyone, but he'd had no intention of staying. He'd promptly pushed the entire visit from his mind and focused on the season and winning races.

Ross ground his teeth together as the rich smell of fermenting corn mash invaded his nostrils. It was a smell that reminded him of home, and of his childhood. It was also, for now, a smell that represented his prison.

He forced that thought away. He couldn't remember the first time he'd ever smelled the mash, but it brought memories crowding into his mind. Memories like running through the distillery until his dad yelled at him to stop. He'd been playing with his brothers and not paying attention. They'd all gotten in trouble, and they'd gotten a lecture. He remembered taking a girl inside once, trying to impress her when they'd been on a date. He also remembered his dad sweating in the fermentation room, beaming with pride over the process that made Blackthorne Gold, their most famous and expensive whisky. People paid a premium for Blackthorne Gold, and Ross was thankful they did.

Gleaming copper tanks perched at regular intervals throughout the room Holly led him through. The wooden floors gleamed. The Blackthorne logo had been painted onto the oak floors as well. The entire place was spotless and beautiful.

Holly Brooks strode through the room like she owned it and led him up a set of stairs. Then they entered a room with a window that looked out over the copper stills below.

A group of men and women sat at the large conference table. Evan Brooks, the master distiller, rose when Ross walked in. "Hello, Mr. Blackthorne. Welcome to the distillery."

Ross shook his hand. "Thank you, Mr. Brooks. You can call me Ross. It's good to see you again."

Evan Brooks nodded. "You too. And call me Evan. Most everyone here does anyway." The man beamed at Holly, who was standing quietly by and looking sweetly accommodating. As if she hadn't basically implied to Ross that he was shallow and she didn't like him. "You've met my niece, Holly. She's going to be your mentor for the next few weeks."

Holly didn't bat an eyelash, but he was pretty sure her eyes hardened to diamond chips. *Great.* "Holly has been nothing but welcoming," Ross said with a smile.

Evan Brooks cleared his throat. Almost as if he'd been worried that Holly might not have been. "That's terrific. Nobody knows this place like Holly. Not even me." Evan gestured to the others standing around the table. "These people are the ones responsible for the day to day work of making the whisky. I thought you might like to meet everyone, and then perhaps another tour to refresh your mind."

"Sounds great."

It didn't sound great, not really, but no way would Ross offend this man who was being so nice to him. All Ross wanted was to get back to the garage and work on his racecar with the team, but that wasn't happening. He had to go through the motions here, like Devlin had said, and then he could go back to doing what he loved.

Or so he hoped. He didn't want to contemplate what would happen if his dad stayed stubborn about this. A vision of himself in an office, wearing a suit, made him shudder. But he kept the smile pasted on his face and shook hands with every person Evan introduced. After the introductions, Evan took Ross on another tour of the distillery. Holly followed along behind for a while and then she excused herself.

By the time the tour was done, Ross's head was swimming with details. He wanted nothing more than to walk out into the parking lot, get into his car, and speed away. Holly reappeared then, coming down the hallway toward them like a breath of fresh air. He focused on her, willing away the despair trying to choke him.

Everyone at the distillery treated him like a rock star. Hell, everyone in general did. Here it was because he was a Blackthorne. Out there it was because he drove a racecar.

But not her. Holly's eyes snapped with dislike. Oddly enough, it grounded him. Everyone else acted like he was supposed to love working in the business, but Holly's eyes said she knew. She *knew* he wasn't cut out for it. That he was going to fail.

He grinned at her and she hesitated for a second. But then she set that look of cool dislike back onto her face and lifted her chin. Her uncle was oblivious to the undercurrents as he greeted her. "Ah, Holly. Can you take Ross and show him some of what you do?"

"Of course."

Evan glanced at his watch. "I've got a meeting with a customer this afternoon. I'll see you both later."

Evan walked away and Ross found himself face to face with Holly. Or face to top of head, more like. She didn't even come up to his chin. She tilted her head up and stared at him. "Having fun?"

He thought about lying. But he decided he wasn't going to. Not to her. She already saw through him, so why bother? "Not particularly."

Her lips thinned.

"I appreciate what you do here," he added. "But I've never wanted to work in the whisky business."

"Fair enough, I suppose."

"It's not my thing."

She held up a hand. "Say no more. You prefer to burn money driving souped up stock cars and setting yourself on fire. I get it. We're boring in comparison."

He felt a pinprick of annoyance. And admiration because, damn, nobody ever talked to him that way. "Everybody needs a hobby," he said with a smile. Because he knew it would only make her madder.

She arched an eyebrow. "Some of us have to work for a

living, Mr. Blackthorne. We don't have the luxury of expensive hobbies."

"I think you do have a hobby, Miss Brooks," he said lightly. "And you excel at it."

"Oh really? What's that?"

He smiled. "Riding your high horse."

———

HOLLY HEARD Uncle Evan in her head, telling her this was her opportunity to impress the Blackthornes—and she was blowing it. Piss off Ross Blackthorne and she'd be lucky to even have a job when she was through, much less ever take over the distillery as master distiller.

It was more than that, however. She'd lashed out at him about things that were none of her business. Spoken in anger just because he wasn't interested in the whisky business and dared to say so. It didn't matter if he was whisky royalty. He didn't have to be interested in being a part of the business, and she had no right to get mad at him about it.

Yeah, she'd lost her family business and missed it every day. But that wasn't Ross Blackthorne's problem or fault.

Holly sucked in a breath. "I shouldn't have said that."

"Which part?"

"Any of it. It's none of my business what you do with your time or your money."

"No, it's not," he said. "But maybe you aren't wrong about me."

"I beg your pardon?"

He shrugged. "I respect the whisky, Holly. Without it, I wouldn't have the opportunities I've had. But I'm not in love with it, not like you and your uncle and everyone here. Not like my dad. I've never wanted to make whisky. I'm a gear head at heart. I want to get my hands dirty tinkering with engines, not cleaning out fermentation tanks. One of those things excites me. The other bores me to tears."

It was an honest answer and she could respect it. Even if she was still determined not to like him. "But the choice isn't yours right now, is it?"

He shook his head. "No, it's not. I crashed on the last lap of a televised race a week ago. It was pretty brutal to look at, I'll admit that. Apparently it made my dad decide I need to give up racing and learn the whisky business."

"Neither of which you want to do."

"No, I don't." He spread his hands. "But I don't have much of a choice in the matter. I'm here and you're stuck with me—at least until my dad will listen to reason."

"And if he doesn't?"

Ross's smile didn't reach his eyes. "Then I guess you'll be stuck with me for a lot longer than either of us wants."

Holly drew herself up. "Okay then. So you're here now and I'm tasked with teaching you how to run this place. I'm not going to pretend to do it while you pretend to pay attention. Therefore, I'd appreciate it if you'd take this seriously for the time being. I have to do the job I've been asked to do."

"I'll do my best," he said softly, his gaze intent on hers.

Holly's heart skipped. Her belly tightened. Why did he have to be so damned good looking? And why did he have to affect her when she knew he was nothing more than a serial womanizer? She thought back to the photos on the internet. Ross surrounded by gorgeous women. He sometimes dated one, but it didn't last long. A handful of photos and then it was over. Models, actresses, debutantes. None of them lasted.

Holly took a step backward, putting space between them. So she could think without a current of heat swirling around her. "See that you do. I'm a busy woman, Ross Blackthorne. I don't have time for games."

He arched an eyebrow. "Are you always so direct? Or is it just me who brings out the best in you?"

Fresh heat flooded her. She hoped like hell she wasn't blushing but she knew it was probably a futile hope with her coloring. "I try to be as direct as possible. I've found it saves a lot of time when people know where they stand."

"And I stand somewhere between a headache and a pain in the ass, right?"

"I didn't say that."

"You didn't have to." He cocked his head as he studied her. "Are you married, Holly?"

Her belly flipped. "What does that have to do with learning how to run a distillery?"

He shrugged. "Nothing at all. Just curious. If I have to spend time with you, I want to know if there's a mister out there who might get pissed about it."

Holly stiffened. "No, I'm not married. Even if I was, it's my damned job to train you—and you need to worry about *me* being pissed off, not some man. I'm in control of my own life, thanks."

"Okay, no husband. Boyfriend?"

"Does it matter?" she asked, grinding her teeth together. "I've already told you I'm the one who makes decisions for me."

"That may be true, but I've found that boyfriends and husbands tend to get a little *extra* annoyed when I'm around."

"Extra annoyed. Like I am right now? It's probably because you're irritating."

He laughed. "Hey, I'm just reporting the facts. I prefer not to have some guy come at me because you're mad and you complain about me when you get home."

"Oh for goodness sake. Look, even if I *did* complain about you when I got home, any man who took that as a sign I needed him to come after you would not be a man I'd be with. I can take care of my own problems, thank you. Now are you ready to get started or do you want to stand here and irritate me some more?"

He shook his head, laughing softly. "Fine, let's get started. But know this, Holly Brooks—I'm going to make you like me before this is over. Guaranteed."

She rolled her eyes. "I don't *dis*like you. I'm just not as impressed with you as you'd like me to be."

"What does that mean exactly?"

"It means I don't care if you're a racecar driver, or rich, or the rightful owner of this distillery. You're just another guy—and I'm not treating you like you're special. You have enough people like that in your life, I'm sure."

"I think I figured that out about you by now," he said, grinning.

She hated when he grinned. He was far too appealing then. "If you're done chatting, let's get to work."

"One condition."

"Do you really think you're in a position to set conditions?"

"Yeah, I do," he told her somewhat arrogantly.

Holly managed not to roll her eyes a second time. Barely. She folded her arms over her chest. "Okay, shoot."

"If I have to learn about running a distillery, I want you to come to my garage and see the cars. Learn something about them."

She stared at him. "Did I mention I was busy?"

"You mentioned it. But it won't take as much time as teaching me about the distillery will. Just come once."

She didn't know why he cared so much but apparently he did. And even though she didn't much like him, in spite of what she'd said about it earlier, if a couple of hours in a garage made him easier to work with, then why not? The more he paid attention, the faster she could go. Then she could be rid of him while he sat in his office and did whatever it was executive vice presidents did.

"Okay. If that's what it takes to make you pay attention to me."

He lifted an eyebrow. "Oh, Holly—trust me, I'm not going to have any trouble paying attention to you."

Chapter 4

Ross had been at the distillery for nearly a week now, following Holly around everywhere and learning more than he cared to about processes.

Today had been a long day in which she'd cut him no slack, and Ross was ready to head back to his home near Louisville and crash with a couple of beers and some Netflix. But first he planned to swing by and check in on Martin and the team before they pulled out for the next race.

He intended to stay in close contact while working at the distillery because nobody—his father in particular—had told him he couldn't. Wasn't going to be easy to walk in there and see the team preparing for a race without him, but he needed that contact with the world he loved.

He exited the building and walked over to the LaFerrari, which he'd driven again today. The parking lot had emptied out for the most part, though there were a handful of cars left. He got inside and started it up, loving the smooth growl of the powerful engine. He glanced up in time to see Holly come outside, phone to her ear, face scrunched in serious concentration. When wasn't she serious?

He had yet to see her do more than crack a grin here and there. In fact, whenever she did smile and he was near, she quickly wiped the smile from her face as if she didn't want him to see her happy.

She'd given him hell this week, but he thought maybe they understood each other a little bit better now. She was a workaholic who loved what she did and she wasn't planning to go easy on him for anything. He'd had to sit through team meetings and product discussions, and he'd learned about ordering the correct charred oak barrels and how long it took for them to come in. There'd been discussions about corn and mash and equipment, and his head was still spinning.

They'd also toured the barrelhouses and he'd listened to her talk about the aging process and which barrels were nearly finished and which were just beginning. She'd glared at him when he'd been unable to tell her which whisky was older. It was the ones at the bottom, which he damned well knew, but he'd been annoyed at how much he liked watching her walk between the aisles while making notes on her clipboard and he'd only half been paying attention.

Every day was something new. Every day was packed. Today had been a full day as well and he was ready to be done. But Holly stopped in mid-stride and put a hand to her forehead, nodding at whoever was on the phone as she did so. He watched with interest as she fumbled in her purse and came up with a set of keys.

Then he waited to see which car she'd unlock. He hadn't stuck around this week to see her leave work so he didn't know. His money was on the champagne Honda Accord sitting nearby. But she walked right past it and over to a white Jeep with the top down. It was an older Jeep, not the sleek models they made now. She slung her purse inside and climbed into the vehicle. A second later, she put the phone down and inserted the key into the ignition.

He couldn't hear the Jeep over the sound of the LaFerrari, but he could tell by Holly's expression that it wasn't starting. She slapped the wheel a couple of times and then put her forehead on it. A moment later, she glanced over at him as if just realizing he was there. He didn't know how she'd missed him but she'd been mighty engrossed in her conversation.

He should leave her there to stew in her meanness but he wasn't that kind of guy. He switched off the ignition and got out of the car.

"It's okay," she yelled at him. "Happens all the time. It'll start in a minute."

"I'll have a look."

She frowned. "You couldn't possibly—"

She stopped talking. Maybe she realized it was silly to imply he couldn't tell what might be wrong, or maybe she'd decided it was futile to protest. Either way, he reached the Jeep and started to unsnap the clips holding the hood down.

"Turn on the lights, Holly."

"Why?"

"Just do it."

He stepped back to have a look. The lights came on. "Not your battery."

"I didn't think it was. It's the starter. It's been kind of wonky lately."

He found the starter and looked at it. He'd need a screwdriver to test the connection, but he didn't have one. He didn't actually want one either so he didn't ask her if she happened to have one inside the Jeep. Instead, he closed the hood and clipped it. "I'll give you a ride home."

Why? She hated him. Why on earth did he want to subject himself to the only female he'd ever met who glared at him instead of batted her eyelashes and smiled?

Holly's mouth dropped. Clearly, she was surprised too. "No. Oh no, I couldn't trouble you. Besides, I need to go to the grocery store and run some errands."

"With a wonky starter?"

"It'll work in a few minutes."

"Why don't you just replace it?"

Her gaze slid past him to the LaFerrari. "I'm sure that's easy for you to say, but a starter and the labor to replace it is about three hundred dollars. Which isn't a ton of money, I'll grant you—but it's also not money I've wanted to spend if I didn't have to."

She was right. Three hundred dollars was nothing much to him, but for someone like her with a job and bills, it was probably a bite out of the budget. "I can put it in for you. That'll save you a few bucks anyway."

She was chewing the inside of her lip. "I don't know."

"Why not? Cars are my thing, babe. I'll be happier replacing your starter than ordering whisky barrels and inventorying supplies."

Her jaw dropped. "Did you just call me *babe?*"

He grinned, enjoying this more than he should. "Guess so."

"Oh. My. God. You're such a player." She crossed her arms and tried to look stern but it didn't really work. Not this time.

"Oh come on, Holly. You can call me babe too if it makes you feel better."

"I'm not calling you anything. Except maybe jerk face."

"Call me whatever you want. Just let me fix your starter."

Her frown deepened. Then she sighed. He knew he

had her then. "Fine. If it makes you happy."

"It does. Now come on, get in my car and I'll take you to the store and home."

"What about my starter?"

"I've got connections. Let me get it for you and you can pay me back." He wouldn't take her money but she didn't need to know that yet.

She twisted the key once more, unwilling to give up so easily. Nothing happened, not even a click. "I can ask one of the guys to take me home."

"You want that starter?"

She gazed up at him with wide eyes. There were fine freckles on her cheeks and her skin was pale and smooth. Her hair was a dark auburn red, rich as the whisky they bottled inside, and lustrous. He imagined spearing his fingers into it. Spreading it across his pillow. His groin tightened.

Another shocker for him since he usually liked women who were more, well, jiggly with the curves.

"Yes," she said.

It took him a moment to remember what he'd asked her. For a brief second, he'd imagined her saying yes to his unspoken thoughts. *Jeez, Ross, get it together.* Devlin and Jason might have taken the plunge into a relationship but that wasn't anything Ross intended to try. Especially not with sassy Holly Brooks.

Besides, it was too much fun being the kind of guy who could take home a different woman every night. And if he had to work here for the foreseeable future, then maybe flirting with Holly wasn't the best idea.

Except he liked flirting with her. He liked seeing her mad at him and then he liked it when she was forced to be nice to him for some reason. It annoyed her so much to be nice to him. "Then you know what you have to do."

She made a face as she grabbed her purse and phone. "This is blackmail," she grumbled as she swung open the door and jumped down. She headed for the LaFerrari without waiting for him. He followed, watching her ass shake the entire way.

Cute little ass. Two perfect handfuls.

"Not yet it isn't," he said beneath his breath.

But he wasn't above a little blackmail if it got him something good. He'd save that for another day.

———

FOR THE SECOND TIME EVER, Holly found herself cradled in the Ferrari. The engine rumbled and purred as Ross smoothly navigated the car out of the parking lot.

"This is a really nice car," she said, feeling all kinds of nervous and out of sorts. Why? She'd spent almost a week with him, forcing him to go over invoices and procedures before dragging him through barrelhouses. She hadn't felt nervous once.

Because you're in your element in the distillery. Out here? You're in uncharted territory, girl.

"It's a special car," he said. "There was a waiting list— and no guarantee I'd get chosen."

Holly gaped at him. "Seriously? You had to throw your name in a hat or something?"

"Something like that. Everything all right?"

"Huh?"

"Your phone call. Looked intense."

She waved a hand as she stared at the red and black dash, the rearing horse logo. "Work. Nothing serious, just a delay on some paperwork we need. This is a really pretty car, by the way. Though I don't know about a waiting list."

He laughed softly. "Pretty. That's just how Ferrari imagined people talking about this car."

She rolled her eyes. "Make fun of me all you want, but it's just a car. A pretty car and an expensive one. But it ultimately doesn't have any purpose beyond other cars. It gets you from point A to point B and back again."

He was still laughing. "You're the first woman I know to sit inside a two million dollar exotic car and call it *just* a car."

Holly's belly dropped. "Two million dollars? For this?"

Oh God, that was unreal levels of rich. And she was riding around with him like they were chummy coworkers or something. Ross Blackthorne didn't just live in a different world than she did. He lived in a different universe.

"Like I said, it's a special car."

"And you drove it to the distillery all week long. What if someone scratched the paint?"

"They'd better not."

"Accidents happen. My God, I'd wrap this thing in bubble wrap and keep it in the garage if I were you."

He snorted. "It's okay, Holly. It's meant to be driven. Would I be upset if it got scratched? Uh, yeah. But it's a risk I'm willing to take. Besides, it's insured."

"I can't imagine what the premiums are."

"You don't want to know."

"No, I really don't."

"So which grocery store am I going to?" he asked as he navigated the streets.

"I'm not sure I want you stopping at any grocery store, quite honestly. Just drop me at home and go wrap this thing up for the night."

"Okay. How about dinner then?"

Holly blinked. "Dinner?"

"Yeah, you know. A meal? I eat, you eat. Food someone else prepares and brings to us?"

"I know what dinner is—but you want to park this thing in a restaurant parking lot?"

He shot her a glance. "Holly. Stop worrying about the car. It's not your responsibility. It's mine. If it gets dinged, then it's my fault. I'm not going to blame you."

She thought about it. She *was* hungry. But she'd been planning to go to the store, pick up a few things, and then head home to eat dinner alone and watch some television before crashing for a few hours. Her bestie had called earlier, wanting to go out tonight, but she'd begged off. Several days with Ross Blackthorne following her around had worn her out. And it wasn't even Friday yet.

Mel found the whole thing hilarious, of course. "Ross Blackthorne?" she'd practically squealed. "The racecar driver? Oh em gee, he's so hot!"

"And he knows it," Holly had grumbled.

"He's not dating anyone right now, you know."

"And that affects me how?"

"Oh come on, Hols—he's gorgeous and you're working with him. He's rich and handsome and—well, you'd be crazy if you didn't try to get some of that."

After Holly had gone on for five minutes about why there was no way in hell she was trying to *get some of that*, Mel had laughed and said, "Fine. If you don't want him, can you introduce me to him?"

"Friends don't let friends date Ross Blackthorne," Holly had said. Mel laughed and then they moved on to other things. And now Holly sat in the man's car, trying to decide if she should take him up on dinner or insist he take her home. If he took her home, the contents of her refrigerator were getting pretty lean, which meant it was probably toast for dinner.

"Earth to Holly," Ross said, and she realized she'd been silent for at least a minute now. "Dinner. Yes or no? And I'm buying, by the way, so feel free to pick the most expensive restaurant in town."

She ought to say no on principal. But toast wasn't really appealing. Her stomach growled as if to punctuate the moment.

"Okay, yes, dinner would be nice. Thanks."

"Great. Where do you want to go?"

She thought about it for a few moments. She could do expensive, soak him for something really great. But hearty and home-cooked was better in her book. And she didn't often care for fancy. "Muriel's has good Southern cooking. If that appeals."

"Sure. Tell me where it is."

The car ride was awkward. They didn't talk much, except for her giving him directions. Finally, they pulled up in front of a little dive with faded blue paint, red shutters, and rusty gates propped against the building. Country decor, she guessed.

Muriel's Diner was written in faded letters across the top. An old sign, the kind you changed the letters on, stood sentinel over the parking lot. *Daily special - fried okra, catfish, hushpuppies, coleslaw - 10.99*

The parking lot was packed, of course. Ross shot her a look. "You're really testing me on the parking lot thing, aren't you?"

"You said you didn't care."

"Okay, I care a little bit. But I'm going to make it work, so don't say a word."

A few minutes later, he'd parked the car at the very end of a row, as far from the next car as possible. The spot had the added bonus of being able to be seen from inside the restaurant, which she discovered when the hostess seated them at a booth by the window. Ross grinned as he opened his menu.

"See. Made it work." He'd put on a ball cap and tugged it down before they came inside, and he sat with his back to as much of the crowd as possible.

It suddenly hit her why. Oh lord, she hadn't thought of that. Ross Blackthorne the racecar driver in a Mom & Pop restaurant that was probably jam-packed with NASCAR fans.

At least the booths were high-backed. It helped. A little.

"I didn't know it would be so crowded," Holly apologized. "I mean I don't usually come here for dinner. Lunch sometimes. It's steady at lunch but never like this."

Ross glanced around the restaurant. It was a typical Southern diner, with cracked vinyl seating, rustic wood paneling, and the kinds of smells that said you wouldn't leave here hungry. She didn't know what he was thinking but she suddenly felt bad that she'd dragged him here. He didn't belong in a place like Muriel's. He belonged in a Michelin-starred restaurant with tablecloths and a sommelier. The kind of place where voices were soft and someone played a piano.

Where a woman with manicured nails and a clingy dress cozied up to him and hung on his every word. Where his presence wasn't likely to cause a stampede when folks realized he was in the room.

"I should have picked something else," Holly said. "I'm sorry."

He met her gaze, his dark eyes flashing with humor. "Don't apologize. It's quaint. And if the food is as good as the crowd seems to suggest, I'm sure I'll be coming back often."

"Really? I wouldn't have thought this was your kind of

place," she said, viewing it through the eyes of a guy who drove a two million dollar car.

"They make really good food, right?"

"Well. Yes."

"Then it's my kind of place."

The waitress appeared at their table. "Hey, Holly, haven't seen you in a month or two."

"Oh, hey, Glenda," Holly said. "How have you been?"

Glenda's husband had worked at the distillery when it was still under the Brooks family's ownership, though he'd since gone to work for another distiller in Bourbon County. She didn't blame him, but she'd hated to lose him.

"Great, hon. How's your sister doin'?"

Fresh despair rolled through Holly at mention of Emily, but she kept a smile on her face. "She's doing okay, thanks for asking."

"Good, good. And Ricky? He enjoying working for that drug company in Connecticut?"

Holly clasped her hands on the table. "Oh sure, Ricky's doing good." Her brother had landed on his feet after the fire that destroyed the warehouses. He'd left the whisky business for good, and left her and Uncle Evan to deal with the aftermath.

"Well, great. What can I get you to drink, hon?"

"Iced tea, thanks."

She turned to Ross. Blinked twice. "Oh my... are you Ross Blackthorne?"

Ross turned on his megawatt smile. "Yes, ma'am. Pleased to meet you," he said, holding out his hand.

She took it, her grin going all goofy. "Oh my word, the grandkids won't believe this. Little Frankie is a huge NASCAR fan. You're his favorite driver."

Holly grew uncomfortable while Glenda peppered Ross with questions. But he answered them all, signed a

napkin for Frankie and his brother David, and ordered a
glass of water by the time it was all done. Several other
patrons looked their way, but nobody else came over to
disturb him. Probably because they couldn't really see him
well and weren't sure if he was somebody important
or not.

"I'm so sorry," Holly said when Glenda sashayed away.
"I really didn't think about anybody recognizing you when
I picked Muriel's."

"It happens." He shrugged. "I don't mind. It comes
with the territory."

Glenda returned with their drinks, gushed some more,
then took their orders. Holly ordered the meatloaf with
mashed potatoes and green beans. Ross ordered chicken-
fried steak with white gravy, biscuits, and collard greens.
Not because he seemed to want collards, but because
Glenda assured him they were the best greens anywhere.

Once she was gone again, Ross turned his attention
back to Holly. She had to admire how he did it. How he
seemed to give whoever was talking to him his full attention, though he had to be trying to figure out how to
escape sometimes.

"So how did you end up in Kentucky?" she asked. "I
thought most NASCAR teams were based in North
Carolina."

He nodded. "They are. But Martin Temple is a
Kentuckian, and he's who I wanted to build my cars and
run my team. He'd retired from the sport until I talked him
into returning. The only way I could do that was come to
Kentucky."

"How do you like it here?"

"I like it a lot, actually. My family lives in Maine and
Boston. It's colder up there. I kind of like being somewhere
that snow isn't really a factor."

"It snows here. You just wait."

"Yeah, but not often. And not several feet at a time."

Holly sipped her iced tea. "No, definitely not several feet. *Brr*," she said, shuddering. "I don't think I'd like that either."

Ross ran his finger up and down the side of his water glass. She didn't know if he was aware he was doing it or not, but she found that the smooth motion distracted her. She wanted to reach out and make him stop. Instead, she looked away. There was a crowd gathering around his car. Naturally.

He followed her gaze. "Can't blame them," he said.

"Nope. You drive around in something like that, you're going to get attention."

"You think I want the attention?"

She swung her gaze to his. "Don't you?"

He shrugged. "Maybe. Classic middle child syndrome. I have two older brothers and one younger one. But I also have three cousins who came to live with us when we were all kids. So, yeah, definitely a middle child. Maybe I'm compensating for it now."

"Compensating for *something*," she said with a smile.

He laughed. "You're hilarious, Holly Brooks. I like you. Even if you don't like me."

He was flirting with her. She kind of liked it. "You're growing on me. Buying me dinner is going a long way to making you seem like a nice guy."

"So you can be bought with food?"

"Sometimes. Like tonight when I was contemplating going home and eating toast for dinner because I really need to get to the store."

"I said I'd take you shopping."

"I know. But that car…" She turned to look at it again. The crowd had moved on but there was a boy, probably a young teenager, standing near the car, trying to see inside without touching it.

"Hang on," Ross said. "I'll be back in a few minutes."

She watched him walk out the door, thinking he was probably going to go over and tell the kid to get away from the car. No doubt there was an alarm or something that was about to go off if the boy got any closer.

Ross walked over and spoke to him. The boy stuck his hand out and they shook. A moment later, Ross was opening doors and letting the teen get inside. Then he stood back to take pictures with the kid's phone.

Holly didn't want to melt. Not at something Ross Blackthorne was doing. But she didn't have any choice in the matter. She watched him let a kid sit in his car and take pictures—second one so far—and she knew she couldn't dislike him. Not really.

He was a good guy. Okay, so he was still a player and all that, but he was decent enough. More than decent enough in some ways.

"That sure is nice of him," Glenda said as she arrived with a tray and started setting food on the table. "That's Billy Truesville. His daddy's been in prison for meth dealing for a year now. Billy washes dishes to help his mama pay the bills."

"He doesn't look old enough to work."

"He'll be sixteen in a month. He can wash dishes after school, which he does three nights a week. It's not a lot, but it helps. Harry pays him under the table." Glenda set the last dish down. "He might or might not know who Ross Blackthorne is, but I guarantee you he won't ever forget him after tonight."

No, he wouldn't.

Holly didn't think she would either.

Chapter 5

Ross spent more time than he'd intended outside, but Billy was so excited about the car and he didn't have the heart to rush the kid. But then Billy announced he had to get to work and headed for the side entrance to the restaurant. Ross sauntered back inside and discovered that Holly hadn't eaten yet. She was sitting with her phone out, scrolling, her food untouched on the table in front of her.

"Sorry," he said as he slid into the booth. "You should have eaten."

She put the phone away and smiled. He liked it when she smiled. He'd rarely been the target of those this week, so it took some getting used to.

"Glenda just brought it a couple of minutes ago. Besides, everything is always served so hot that letting it cool a little is no big deal."

"Still, I'm sorry I took so long. Billy had a lot of questions."

Holly opened a paper napkin and put it on her lap. "It was nice of you to do that."

He unfolded his own napkin. The food smelled delicious. "When I was a kid, I loved cars. I wanted Hot Wheels all the time. Then I wanted models and remote controlled cars when I got a little older. More than that, I wanted a Corvette. That was my dream car for the longest time. Whenever I'd see one somewhere, I wanted to look at it. Most of the people who had them let me. There were some who didn't. Some who were rude or irritated. I never forgot what that felt like. I won't do that to a kid."

Holly was watching him with a frown on her face. "How old were you?"

"The first time? Twelve or thirteen, I think. An old guy with a red C3—that's the model. They run C1 through C8. But he had a C3 and I wanted to talk to him about it. He told me to get lost."

"That wasn't nice."

Ross shrugged. "No, but I was a kid. Who knows if he was busy or had somewhere to be—I was upset about it back then, but I kinda get it now. Anyway, whenever a kid wants to see my car, I let him. Or her. It's not always boys."

She dropped her gaze to her plate and pushed her food around. He wondered if he'd said something wrong. "How's your food?" she asked when she looked up again.

"It's great." He took a bite of the biscuit he'd buttered. "Damn I love biscuits. I mean we have biscuits in Maine, but they don't taste the same."

"It's the flour," she announced. "Southern cooks use White Lily flour. It's softer."

"Whatever it is, it works." He polished off the biscuit and took another bite of the chicken-fried steak with white gravy. Another Southern dish he'd learned to love when Martin had introduced him to it at a Cracker Barrel in Louisville one night. "What did you love as a kid, Holly?"

She seemed surprised. "Love?"

"I loved cars. What did you love?"

"Oh, well." She grinned. "Horses. I was a typical horse-crazy girl. Lexington is amazing horse country. I took lessons for a while, showed a little bit. I had a horse but I had to sell him when I went to college."

"Do you still ride?"

"No time these days, unfortunately."

"Maybe you should make time. If you love it."

"It's not that easy."

"Why not? You don't work every hour of the day."

She sighed. "Horses take a lot of time. And they cost a lot—board, feed, vet bills, shoeing. I can't justify the expense."

That wasn't something he could argue with. Not everyone could afford to spend money on hobbies. Especially not expensive ones. He took a sip of his drink. "Glenda mentioned you have a brother and a sister."

He thought her jaw tightened for a moment. But then she smiled. It didn't reach her eyes. "Yes."

"Older? Younger?"

"Ricky is the oldest. Emily is the youngest."

"So you're a middle child too."

"I am."

Ross sighed. "I'm making conversation here, Holly. If you don't want to talk about your family, give me something else to go on."

She closed her eyes for a second. Then she shook her head. "I'm sorry. It's just that my family went through a lot when the barrelhouses burned. Ricky and Emily worked in the distillery. But Ricky left after, and Emily…"

He'd heard Glenda ask about her sister, and she'd said her sister was fine. But there was clearly something that upset her. "It's okay. You don't have to tell me."

"No, I know. But maybe you should hear it. You're going to hear it anyway, and I'd rather it was from me than someone else in the distillery. I'm kinda surprised you haven't by now."

"I haven't. I don't know what you're talking about." But he could tell it was hard for her to say it.

She huffed in a breath. Blew it out. "Emily suffered brain damage during the fire. She was running—we all were—to help. Not that we could have done anything, but we were going to try. There was whisky and water everywhere and it was slippery. She fell and a barrel slammed into her, knocking her unconscious. We didn't think it was so serious—but she was in a coma for a month—and when she came out again we learned she'd suffered irreparable brain damage."

HOLLY'S CHEST WAS TIGHT. Her stomach roiled. Her food was no longer appealing. She put her fork down and crossed her arms. Why was she even telling him this? And how was she going to stop herself from crying right here in front of Ross Blackthorne and everyone?

He set his fork down. His face contained so much sympathy. In that moment, she was suddenly terrified of him. When Ross Blackthorne was just a playboy and a daredevil, she could compartmentalize him. Keep him firmly in the category of *Go there, Don't.*

When he let kids sit in his outrageously expensive sports car and then showed sympathy over her sister's accident, he became too human. He was nice, kind, and so handsome it hurt to look at him. She didn't want to like him, or think well of him. She wanted him to stay in his box, the one where he tried to get into as many panties as he could and didn't give a shit about anyone but himself.

"I'm sorry, Holly. That had to be so hard for your family."

She sucked in a breath. Bit the inside of her lip. She would *not* cry. Not now. "It was," she breathed.

"How is she now?"

"She's good. Really. She can't live alone, so she lives in a group home for people who can't live alone, but she's learned to do many of the things she once could. It's just…" Holly squeezed her arms against her body. It hurt so much to think of all Emily had lost. "She'll probably never get married, you know? Never have a relationship with a man. No kids or, hell, just going out for a girls' night with friends."

"Everything changed for you—your whole family—when the whisky burned."

"Yes."

"How did you end up selling to my father?"

Holly's heart hurt. "We were pretty much wiped out. We tried to get enough whisky from other distilleries to see us through. That happens sometimes—have a loss, buy whisky and label it as your own until you can recover. But nobody had enough, and customers started to cancel. It was a perfect storm of events, really. My dad had a heart attack and died, my sister was in the hospital learning how to feed herself again, and we were all just tired and desperate, I think. Your father offered to buy. It was a really good deal for us, especially since Uncle Evan and I got to stay. Ricky could have stayed, but he chose not to."

Like Ross, Ricky had never cared for the whisky business. It wasn't in his blood the way it was in hers. To him, it'd just been another job. She even thought, though she'd never said it aloud, that he was relieved the distillery had to be sold. It gave him an out.

"I hope that moving under the Blackthorne label hasn't been too difficult."

For her personally, yes, because of everything she'd lost. Professionally? No.

"Blackthorne has been good to us. We've expanded quickly, hired more workers, and our product line is growing. Well, *your* product line. I still think of the distillery as my family legacy, though it's not anymore."

And that was the hard part, really. She'd always known she was going to grow up to be a whisky maker. Then she was going to inherit the distillery with her brother and sister someday. Uncle Evan and Aunt Brenda were childless, but Holly and her siblings would carry on the traditions.

Only now they wouldn't. Ricky was in Connecticut, Emily would never work in the distillery again, and Holly wasn't going to inherit a thing. She could make whisky for the Blackthornes, but it would never be hers. She wouldn't pass it down to her future children—or probably even teach them to make whisky. No, she'd insist they do something else for a living.

"My family is very proud of their legacy, too," Ross said. "I think my dad would be happy to know how much you still care for the distillery, though it's not your family's anymore. And I'm sorry for that, Holly. For everything that happened to your family with the fire and the aftermath."

Holly pushed away the gloom and pasted on a smile. "That's life, right? And you didn't come to dinner to listen to me complain."

"I didn't think you were complaining. And besides, I asked."

She nodded toward his plate. "You've still got some chicken-fried steak left."

"You've got meatloaf."

Her stomach refused to accept another bite. "I'm going to get a go-box from Glenda. Take this to work for lunch tomorrow."

Ross frowned. "You were eating fine until I asked about your family."

She waved a hand, dismissing his concerns. "Nah, I was getting full anyway."

He finished his food, she got a box for hers, and then he paid. She tried to offer him money, but he refused to take it. "I told you I was buying. Don't argue."

"Then I'll get the next one."

He arched an eyebrow. "Deal."

"What? That fast?"

He grinned at her as he held the door open so she could exit the restaurant. "Yep, that fast. Because you just agreed to go out with me again."

Holly stopped on the steps and blinked up at him. "Oh hell, I did, didn't I?"

"Yep." He put his hand against the small of her back and escorted her to the car. "And don't think I'm letting you out of it, either."

———

IT WAS an hour's drive back to Louisville. Ross put the LaFerrari in the garage and went inside. He'd thought about Holly on the drive back, about the sadness in her eyes when she'd spoken of her sister and the loss of the distillery.

It brought home to him the difference between them. To him, the whisky was just one facet of his family's business—and not one he wanted to participate in. To Holly, the whisky was personal. Her family had been in the same position his was in when his great-grandfather came to this country and started making whisky. The Brookses had been building, growing, looking forward to the day when they sat atop an empire—but the day never came because they lost it all.

Ross couldn't get Holly's face out of his head. The despair in her eyes when she'd talked about her sister. When he'd met her again earlier this week, he'd thought she was pretty. The fact she hadn't liked him made her even more interesting. He wasn't accustomed to that.

But then he spent time with her, saw her care and professionalism first hand, and then learned about the accident that ruined her family—and something deep inside began to gnaw at him. Some unsettled feeling that hadn't dissipated yet.

Ross went over to the bar set against one wall in the kitchen and poured two fingers of Blackthorne Gold, neat. He didn't actually drink much whisky, but when he wanted it, there was only one kind. He thought of his grandmother, Fiona Blackthorne. She was eighty-six, feisty as hell, and she could drink him under the table any day of the week. That thought always made him smile. Which was a good thing right now.

Ross took out his phone and dialed Martin Temple. He needed to stay grounded in the world he knew because he didn't intend to stay at the distillery any longer than he had to. Not even for pretty eyes in a pretty face.

Temple answered on the first ring. "Hello, Ross."

"Hey, Martin." He took a sip of the whisky. It went down smooth, burning on the finish. There were hints of smoke, vanilla, and caramel. "How's it going?"

"Practices have been great. Eric's doing a hell of a job. New engine purrs like a kitten."

A very loud, growly kitten, he imagined. "He's ready for Joliet?"

"He's ready."

"The Quaker State 400 is almost here. I really want to be the one behind the wheel."

"Unless you get your father to tell me otherwise, it'll be Eric."

Ross took another sip. If he didn't drive again soon, he could probably kiss the Cup goodbye. Not that his father cared about that. But it was something Ross had wanted since he was a kid watching NASCAR on television. It'd been the Winston Cup back then. These days it was the Monster Energy Cup. In a few years, maybe it'd be the Blackthorne Cup. "I'll work on him."

"You do that."

They talked about a few other things and then Ross ended the call. He'd finished the whisky by then. He did not get another. He wasn't Fiona and he wasn't about to try.

He thought about calling his brother, Trey. Trey was the eldest and worked closely with their father at Blackthorne Enterprises. If anyone might know what Dad was thinking, it'd be Trey. But sometimes Ross felt like his brother was a carbon copy of Dad, with his seriousness and his dedication to the family business.

No, Trey wasn't who he needed to talk to right now.

He needed to talk to his cousin Brock. Brock was the senior vice president for brand management, which meant he kept close tabs on all things Blackthorne. That also meant he had resources for finding information.

Ross hit the number and waited.

"Ross, holy shit. It's good to hear from you," Brock said.

"Hey, Brock. How's it going?"

"Man, I didn't flip a flaming car while going two-hundred miles an hour, so I guess I'm just fine. How about you? Uncle Graham sent a group text and told us all that you were okay. You couldn't have managed that yourself?"

"Sorry," Ross said as guilt crept through him. "I should have. But Dad called me when I was still being checked out by medical—and he managed to piss me off badly enough I didn't think to text anybody."

Ross had gotten texts from so many people that he'd just sort of expected that's how it was going to go. He should have sent his own texts—or made his own calls—though. Especially since the wreck was nearly two weeks ago.

"Yeah, well I heard about that. And I understand why you're pissed. But dude, next time call and let us know you're not dying."

"Did you see the wreck?"

"Not when it happened, thank God. I was working on something and got called away. By the time I got back to it, I'd heard about the crash and that you were okay through Uncle Graham's text."

"So then you went and watched it on You Tube, am I right?"

"Well, yeah. That was pretty spectacular, Ross. Scary as hell, I bet."

"I mean it's not fun when it's happening—but the cars are safe. There's fire retardant that sprays the car from inside the frame, and we wear fire suits. It gets hot, but we're safe for long enough to get out."

Typically. Things could go wrong, but so far they hadn't.

"Sure, whatever you say. I'm sorry it happened though. You were about to win."

"Seemed like it—but even that could have changed on the last lap."

"Guess so." Brock sighed. "So when do you head for the distillery?"

"I've been there since last Thursday."

"Wow. Didn't expect it to happen so fast, but it's not like Uncle Graham to waste time, is it?"

"Nope. He wasted no time in ordering me to report to the distillery and give up racing for good. Won't even let me finish the season."

"Yikes. He didn't give us details, just said you were going to work at the distillery. I kind of assumed it'd be in a couple of months at least. But we've been needing someone down there and I guess he figured it might as well be you."

"You don't need anyone down here, Brock. The place is being run by people who know exactly what they're doing. Far more than I do."

"Yeah, but they aren't Blackthornes. We need a Blackthorne on staff."

Ross banged his head on the back of the couch. His cousin was obsessive about the Blackthorne name and brand and how it was portrayed in the media. Having a Blackthorne at the Kentucky distillery would make a lot of sense to Brock. "So you approve of Dad's decision?"

"To make you leave racing? No, not really. The NASCAR team gets a lot of eyeballs on the brand. Eyeballs we might not get through other media. It's sexy and daring and people like it."

"It's expensive, though."

"Yeah, it's expensive. But it works."

"So can you tell Dad that for me? Please?" Ross laughed because he knew his dad wasn't going to listen to anyone right now. Not even Brock. Graham Blackthorne was like a lion with a thorn in his paw since Mom had left him.

"I have told him. It's why we still have the team. But he doesn't think you need to be driving for it to work. We have other drivers."

"No, he thinks I need to be executive vice president of Blackthorne Kentucky, right? Just so long as I stay out of Evan Brooks's way—and Holly Brooks, too."

"Ah, the Brooks family. By all accounts, they're an asset to the operation."

"I believe that. Look, that's what I'm calling you about."

"Oh yeah?"

"The fire that destroyed their warehouses. Did you know that the youngest daughter, Emily Brooks, was injured in the fire? Brain injury. She's in a group home."

"I knew there was a fire. I don't think I knew about Emily. I'm sure the information is available, but I didn't go over more than the basics. So what is it you want to know?"

Ross frowned. He thought of the aching sadness in Holly's eyes. The way she'd said her sister would never have a life of her own. Never get married. "I want to know the extent of her injuries. Her prognosis. What kind of facility is she in? What have they done for her? What else could be done?"

"It's not quite my area, but I can put somebody on that. You should be aware we may not learn much though. HIPAA restricts the kinds of things you can find out about a patient."

He hadn't thought about that. "Okay."

"Why do you want to know?"

There was a knot in his throat. "I just wanted to know that every option has been explored."

"You've been there a few days. How have you gone this deep already? You don't even know these people."

"I'm not quite sure. But I want to know about Emily. Can you get me the info?"

"I'll do the best I can. Be next week probably."

"Thanks."

"Sure."

"Hey," Ross added. "Have you figured out what the secret is that Mom said she'd been keeping all these years for Dad?"

Ross had been late to Mom's birthday party and he'd missed the part where she'd yelled at her husband and stormed off, but it's all anyone had talked about after it happened. The speculation had run rampant about what the secret could be. Theft, fraud, infidelity, criminal activity —it ran the gamut, and Ross mostly ignored it all. No sense getting worked up about something they didn't yet know. That was Brock's job. Besides, if anyone was going to figure it out, it'd be Brock.

"No, I haven't. I'm keeping a close eye on the rumor mill, which has some key accounts buzzing, as usual."

Ross could hear the tightness in his cousin's voice. Brock took all potential threats to the Blackthorne brand personally. And very, very seriously.

"It might not be much of anything, you know."

"That's what I'm hoping."

"Thanks for the help, Brock."

"Anytime. I'll let you know what I find out. And Ross?"

"Yeah?"

"I'm really glad you're okay."

"Me too."

The call ended and Ross sat there for a long minute, thinking about Holly Brooks and the distillery. It hadn't been completely torturous so far. Spending time with Holly could be fun, especially when she glared at him when he said or did something nice for her. He didn't know why that amused him, but it did.

Holly wasn't like other women. She was determined not to like him, unlike most of the women he encountered. He knew he was a good-looking guy, but even if he weren't, it wouldn't have mattered. The Blackthorne name opened doors, made people rush to offer him whatever he might want because they hoped they'd benefit somehow.

With women, those offers usually turned personal. Flirtatious. Brock was against one-night stands for reputation's sake, but Ross didn't have the same thought about that as his cousin. In his opinion, it wasn't a stain on the Blackthorne name to enjoy the charms of an attractive woman when she offered them.

But Holly Brooks wasn't offering. Hell, she was barely friendly. Until tonight, when she'd let him glimpse her without the shields and hostility. He wasn't sure what had changed to allow her to be open with him, but he was glad for it.

He wanted more of that Holly.

And he was willing to do just about anything to get it.

Chapter 6

Holly's phone rang early. She was still on her first cup of coffee when the call came. She picked it up, surprised to see that it was Ross Blackthorne. Of course he had her number because it was part of the distillery management contact information he'd been given, but it was the first time he'd used it.

Maybe he was calling in sick so he could get out of coming to work today.

"Hello?"

"Morning, sunshine," he rumbled with that too sexy voice of his.

Sunshine?

"Morning, jerk face."

He laughed. "I didn't call you babe."

"No, but sunshine isn't that much better."

He was still laughing. "Okay, no nicknames at all. No sunshine, sweetie, or babe. No doll or hon. Got it."

"What do you need, Ross?"

"Need?"

His voice dropped an octave. Heat settled between her

legs. It shocked her more than it should. He *was* sexy. She'd have to be dead not to react.

It was just that she didn't *want* to react. Not to Ross Blackthorne of all people. He might be at the distillery now, but he wasn't planning to stay. She didn't delude herself that he was going to, even with his father currently making him work there. Eventually, they'd come to an understanding and Ross would be gone again.

"Yes, why are you calling me? You must need something. Sick today? Can't make it? What?"

"Damn, girl—excuse me—*Holly*. You don't have much of an opinion about my work ethic, do you?"

"I'm just going on what you said. You'd rather be in your garage than at the distillery. So I thought maybe you weren't coming in today."

"I would rather be at my garage. But I'm also a Blackthorne, and we don't quit. My dad wants me at the distillery, that's where I'm going to be every day until I can make him see reason. I was calling to ask if you needed a ride in today."

Heat flared in her cheeks. She was so glad he wasn't here to see it. Way to be an ass, Holly! "Oh, no. Thank you. I was just going to take an Uber."

"Don't bother. I can swing by. The ride is free, unlike Uber."

"I'm not destitute, Ross. I do get a salary."

"Yeah, but you have a starter to pay for, remember?"

Shit. "I do, yes."

"So I've got it with me and I'm on the way. I'll pick you up in half an hour. Is that enough time?"

Holly blinked. "You're on the way to work already?" It was only six a.m. He didn't have to be there until eight.

"No, I'm on the way to pick you up and take you to breakfast."

"No way. You bought dinner last night."

"That's right, I did. It's your turn to pay. Where can we get some really good pancakes?"

"Muriel's. Or just about any Mom & Pop place on the way to the distillery." She said it because she figured he wouldn't want a parking lot repeat in his fancy car.

"So you'll be ready?"

Holly's heart tripped in her chest. He wasn't giving up? And now her palms were sweating. This was ridiculous. "I feel like you aren't giving me a choice here," she said, trying to maintain some semblance of control over the situation.

"You always have a choice, Holly. If you don't want breakfast, we won't go—but fair warning I'm doing the drive through at McDonald's if not. I don't see how you can turn down a free ride to work though. Especially from the man in possession of your starter."

"You have my starter? Already?"

"I said that earlier." He laughed. "Picked it up from a buddy this morning."

Oh geez, he had said it. She remembered now. "How much is it?"

"I have to look at the receipt. I'll let you know later."

She rolled her eyes. Rich people. "When can you put it in?" The minute she said the words, she wished she could call them back. It sounded so... dirty. It shouldn't be dirty. It was just a starter for heaven's sake, and you put starters into cars. But Ross wasn't saying anything and...

Holly touched her cheek. Oh God, her face was on fire right now. What the hell?

"Whenever I get a chance, Holly," he said, his voice rumbly again. Was he flirting with her? Was there a subtext here? Or was she just crazy? "I'd love to put it in as soon as possible."

Oh jeez, definitely a subtext. And yet her body was doing a little dance inside as fireworks ricocheted through her, concentrating between her thighs. She felt all tingly. Hot. Needy.

"Fine," she said as coolly as she could manage. "I'll be ready when you get here."

Holly! Jeez!

He laughed again and she wanted to bury her head under the covers and never come out. "See you soon."

The connection ended and Holly shot to her feet. She ran for the shower, soaped and rinsed her body and washed her hair, then got dressed in record time. She barely had time for mascara before her doorbell rang. Her hair was still damp and she scraped it back into a ponytail. Then she shook her head at herself and went to answer the door.

Ross stood on her front porch, looking like sex on legs in his dark denim jeans and pale lavender Oxford shirt with the cuffs rolled up. He smiled and her belly dipped into her toes.

"Hey. You ready?"

"I have to get my purse," she told him. "And check to make sure I turned everything off."

He stepped inside the entry of her small cottage and hooked his thumbs in his jeans. He looked all casual and sexy, like a guy you'd meet at the feed store or, haha, the racetrack. She had to remind herself that he was wealthy, that he had a two million dollar car sitting outside right now, and that the only reason he was here was because his father had forced him to work at the distillery. The casual look was a ruse. This man could burn one hundred dollar bills to keep warm and not miss a single one.

"Nice place," he said as she went over to pick up her purse from the console table in the hallway. The door opened into a small hall, but the living room opened to the left. It was an older house with the kind of period details she loved. Wainscoting, crown and dentil moldings, and built-in bookcases.

"Thanks. I bought it about a year ago now." She'd grown tired of living in apartments and decided it was finally time to get her own place. She'd gone modest because she never knew when she'd need money for Emily's care. So far her sister was taken care of, but there was very little room for any experimental treatments if they came available. Holly had decided that was a bridge she'd cross if she ever came to it. If she had to sell, she would.

"It's nice."

"Probably a bit smaller than you're used to."

"It's not the size that matters," he said.

Holly didn't say anything about that statement, though she wanted to. Instead, she smiled brightly—and hoped she wasn't turning beet red. "I'll be right back. Have to check I turned off the coffee pot.

"I'll wait," he said with a cocky smile.

She was pretty sure she'd turned it off, but the truth was he turned her brain to mush and she needed to make certain she had. Plus she needed a moment to regroup and refocus.

He was still standing there looking like every woman's fantasy come true when she returned. "All good?" he asked.

"Yep, all good."

He led the way outside. When she turned from locking the door, there was a huge pickup truck in her driveway. It was black. Everywhere. Body, windows, wheels, handles—except for two large gray stripes that went from the hood and up over the cab. There was also a silver snake on the grill. She looked at Ross. He arched an eyebrow and pressed a button on the remote to start the engine. Then he unlocked the doors.

"Where's the car?"

"Disappointed?"

"Not at all. But I wasn't expecting a truck."

"This isn't just any truck, Holly. It's a Ford F-150 Shelby Super Snake."

She shook her head. "I don't even know what that means."

"Performance," he said. "Horsepower. Seven-fifty-five, to be precise."

"You like fast vehicles, don't you?" That was an understatement for sure.

He walked her over to the truck and opened her door. "Yes, ma'am, I sure do."

"Thank you—but I can get my own door next time."

"I know you can." He closed the door as she buckled into her seat. The interior was black and gray, sleek. Gorgeous and new, of course.

Ross got in and snapped his seat belt. "So where do you want to go for breakfast?"

She'd been planning to tell him that a drive-through was fine, but pancakes *would* be awesome, wouldn't they?

"There's a diner on the way to the distillery. They're only open for breakfast and lunch. Ted's Diner."

"Ted's it is," he said, reversing out of the drive. When they got to a stop light on the main road, another car pulled up beside them and two guys hooted. Holly jerked her head toward the sound. The guys were giving Ross a thumbs up.

"Wow, they recognize you already? Through those tinted windows?"

He laughed. "No. It's the truck. It's a Super Snake. That gets guys excited."

"You're kidding."

He shot her a look. "I'm really not. Hang on," he said when the light changed.

Holly squeaked as he floored it and the truck roared off the line. "Are you crazy? It's fifty-five here!"

"And I'm doing fifty-five," he said, backing off the accelerator. "We just got there fast."

"Oh Lord," she muttered. "Do you ever drive like a normal person?"

"I drive *better*," he replied. "I've spent years learning how."

They came up to another stoplight. The car pulled up beside them again. The guys hooted and gave thumbs up. Ross powered the window down.

"Man, that is one cool truck," one of the guys said.

"Thanks," Ross replied.

"You smoked us back there. That was awesome. Can you do it again? Love the way that engine sounds."

"It's good and growly, right?" Ross asked. "Can't do it again though. Scares my lady too much."

"Aw, man. Okay. Seriously cool though."

After Ross powered the window up again, he turned to her. "Before you get mad at me for calling you my lady, it was the simplest way to tell them I wasn't stomping it again."

Holly's heart was busy pitter-pattering in her chest. Not only from the speed but yes, from the fact he'd called her his lady—and she'd liked the way it sounded. Which was seriously worrisome because she knew better. Ross Blackthorne wasn't going to settle for one woman when his money and good looks got him as many as he wanted— and even if he was, it wouldn't be her. It'd be some gorgeous actress or model, not a woman who smelled like fermenting corn mash half the time.

"It's okay. I get it. But, Ross, can I ask you a question?"

"Sure."

"Why are you so nice to everyone? I mean I understand letting the kids sit in your car. But those men weren't kids and you don't owe them a thing. You could have ignored them entirely."

"You think I shouldn't be nice?"

"That's not what I mean. I just mean that whenever people want a piece of your time, you seem to give it to them with no reservations."

He looked serious. "I've had a lot of advantages in this life. Things I didn't work for or earn. Of course I've worked hard to be a race driver, and I've worked hard to build my team and grow it into something worthy of winning the Cup." He made the turn that would eventually take them to Ted's and then the distillery. "But I was born into wealth and privilege, and those guys weren't. If gunning this engine makes them happy, then it doesn't cost me anything to do it. If talking to me about the truck makes them happy, again, doesn't cost me anything but a little bit of time. I can afford that."

His phone rang before she could say anything. Probably a good thing because she didn't know *what* to say.

She stared at the rolling bluegrass fields dotted with sleek, shiny horses. She hadn't wanted to like this man. Not at all.

But she did. And it was vital she didn't let him know it.

━━

FOR THE SECOND time in twenty-four hours, Ross found himself eating a meal with Holly. He didn't know why he'd called her up so early and told her he wanted to go to breakfast, but the truth was that he'd spent half the night thinking about her long red hair, her freckles, and her blue-gray eyes that snapped fire at him no matter how hard he tried to flirt with her.

Holly Brooks was an anomaly in his world. And he was like one of those monkeys in an experiment where he just kept pressing the button, never knowing whether he'd get a shock or a treat. She was addicting in a way—and she didn't even know it.

Right now, she was busy delicately cutting a piece off her ham and cheese omelet. She lifted the chunk to her mouth and blew on it. He focused on those pink lips, the way they puckered, and felt the ache all the way into his groin.

"Good?" he asked as she slipped the food into her mouth.

She blinked at him like she'd forgotten he was there. "Yes, of course. How about yours?"

He'd ordered a big stack of pancakes with bacon and scrambled eggs. He could hear his mother in his head, warning him about cholesterol, but he wasn't too worried about it. He usually ate pretty well, mostly because he had a chef who cooked for him, but when left to his own devices on the road or during dinner meetings with Martin Temple, he liked to eat the fattiest, worst food in the world for his arteries.

And this artery-clogging food was delicious.

"It's every bit as good as you said."

She smiled, and his groin tightened again. Seriously? Cozying up to a hornet nest would probably be easier. And yet he couldn't help his reaction. Holly Brooks was doing it for him. Big time.

"It is good. But I can't keep eating like this or I'm going to gain twenty pounds."

"You'd still be pretty if you did."

Her eyebrows shot up. Then she frowned. Ah, there was the Holly he knew. Hornet nest was putting it mildly.

"Don't you dare flatter me, Ross Blackthorne. I'm not some skinny model you're seeing. You don't have to stroke my ego."

He'd like to stroke something else. He didn't say it though. "You know what, Holly B, I'm not flattering you. I don't *have* to flatter you—and I like that. You say what you mean and you don't care what I think. So I'm saying it back. You're pretty and you'd still be pretty even if you gained twenty pounds."

She gaped at him. He could see the moment the blush happened. It spread from her slender throat like a flower in bloom, opening up over her cheeks and unfurling across her nose. Her gaze dropped. She looked flustered.

Interesting. And good for him.

"Well," she said, spearing more of her omelet as if she didn't have a care in the world. "Thank you. But then I'd have to buy new clothes, so I'm going to have to go back to watching what I eat."

"Maybe we can eat here once a week. Breakfast meetings." He grinned as he forked up a bite of fluffy pancakes.

"Breakfast meetings? About what?"

"Business—barrels. Invoices. Corn. I don't know. Whatever we need to talk about."

She arched an eyebrow. "Speaking of corn, what are the chances of us getting some of that sugar gold from Maine?"

He felt everything inside him cool. He was flirting with her. Hard core flirting with her—and she was thinking about whisky. Of course.

"I don't know. I'd have to call Dad. Or maybe Trey. Though Dad still makes all the decisions, much to Trey's frustration."

"Trey?"

"My brother. He's the oldest. Graham Wallace Blackthorne III, also known as Trey. He's the one who'll take over the business someday. If Dad lets go, that is." He took a bite of bacon. "I wouldn't get too hopeful, though. Sugar gold is what we use to make our premier whisky, and they probably won't want to let any go. Blackthorne Gold is exclusive for a reason."

Holly made a disappointed face. "I just wanted to experiment a little. Not make Gold. I know we aren't meant to do that. Yet."

"Or ever," Ross said. "I don't know the plans for Blackthorne Kentucky, not in their entirety, but I doubt my father or brother will ever turn over the production of our finest whisky to anyone but our distillery in Maine. Tradition you can taste is more than just a slogan. It's everything to my family."

"I'm aware. I've worked for Blackthorne for nearly three years. We had to watch videos, you know. About your great-grandfather and how the distillery started. About the traditions being carried on from generation to generation. And about how the Kentucky site would fit into the Blackthorne brand. We are solidly Blackthorne, believe me."

She didn't say it with malice or regret. He was glad for that. He knew that losing her family distillery had been difficult. "How does our whisky process differ from Brooks Creek?"

She sighed as she picked up her coffee. "It mostly doesn't. Bourbon is bourbon, though there are of course subtle flavor differences between distilleries or why would we all be doing this? But your Blackthorne Gold—now that is something very fine. It's the corn—and the water and the location. Our water comes from our spring-fed creek that filters through limestone rock. Your water up there is different."

He nodded. "I've heard my dad talk about the water. We distill it ourselves from various sources. The water is clear and cold and pure."

"So even if we attempted Blackthorne Gold here, there would be subtle differences. But who knows, those differences might be worthwhile. And I'd certainly like to try one of these days. We could call it Blackthorne Kentucky Gold."

"It's an interesting idea." Ross stabbed more pancakes. "How about that, we've just had our first breakfast meeting."

Holly laughed. "Okay, fine. So does that mean I get to claim this as a business expense?"

"Oh no," he told her, shaking his head. "I'm buying breakfast on the business account."

"But it's my turn."

"Nope, you still owe me a meal. If you hadn't asked about the corn, this wouldn't have gone off the rails. But you did, so here we are."

She stared at him. Then she laughed, a soft giggly sound that he wanted to hear more of. "You're a nut, you know that? In fact, I don't think you ever intended to let me buy breakfast. You want to keep me on the hook for a meal so you can get me to show you all the best food places in Lexington and Bourbon County."

"Maybe I do. I like food."

"I like food too. But I'm about to start taking you to the healthy restaurants for the sake of my buttons." In spite of that statement, she ate another bite of her omelet. It was a huge thing, fluffy, and there were hash browns too.

"You could eat healthy here if you really wanted. They had egg whites on the menu. Spinach. Hell, maybe they even have quinoa. You could have a quinoa omelet."

She made a face. "Oh God, that sounds awful. No."

"Guess you aren't all that dedicated," he teased.

"Not if it involves quinoa omelets. I can tolerate a lot of things, but I don't think that's one of them."

"You're tolerating me," he pointed out.

"Barely." She smiled when she said it though. He liked her smile. It was a little crooked, one corner of her mouth higher than the other. Her lips were lush, and her teeth were small and straight.

He'd like to kiss that mouth. Coax it open so he could slip his tongue between her lips, see if she tasted as sweet as she looked.

"Admit it," he said, "I'm not so bad."

Her gaze dropped to her plate for a second. She pushed her hash browns around. "No," she finally said. "You aren't."

It wasn't much of a statement—but coming from Holly it was a lot.

Ross stabbed another forkful of pancakes, feeling suddenly buoyant inside. "Told you you're going to like me. It's just a matter of time."

"It's only been a few days," she said wryly. "I'm going to need more time than that."

"Lucky for you, I've got nothing but time."

At least until he could get his father to agree that the racing team needed him back. Once that happened, there'd be no more breakfast meetings with Holly Brooks. He'd be back to racing—and Holly would be nothing more than a pleasant memory.

That thought ought to cheer him up. Somehow, it didn't.

Chapter 7

Holly's cell phone rang right before lunch. It was Mel. "Hey, girlie," her bestie said when she answered. "How's it going with that sexy racecar driver?"

Holly leaned back in her chair and smiled. She didn't mean to smile but damned if it didn't happen anyway. "It's going," she replied.

It was definitely going. She'd been to dinner and breakfast with the man, and she'd spent most of the past week with him. He was in his office now—the office the staff had cleared out for him at Uncle Evan's direction—and she could finally breathe again.

Ross Blackthorne sucked all the air out of the room when he was around. He was just so *there*. His presence was becoming more overwhelming to her, not less. She didn't know why that was. Or why she wanted more of the same.

Thank God today was the last day of work for the weekend. Blackthorne Kentucky worked four-day weeks every other week in summer. It was good for morale and it gave the employees time off for errands and family events.

76

"What does that mean, Hols? Going good? Going bad? Going *oohlala*?"

Holly laughed. "It means he's here and I have to train him. It also means my Jeep died yesterday and Ross took me to dinner and home. Then he picked me up this morning and took me to breakfast."

"You. Are. *Kidding* me! Dinner *and* breakfast with Mr. Sexy Racy Pants? What's he like? Is he really as hot in person as he is in pictures? Is he a total jerk or what?"

"Geez, Mel, slow down. I barely know him." She studied the wall across the room. There was a calendar on it with dates marked for production schedules. Of course it was online too, but she really liked having a visual so she could look up and see the entire schedule whenever she wanted. "He's not a total jerk. He seems nice enough, though he's also a Blackthorne and that means he's got a *lot* of money. We went to dinner in a two million dollar Ferrari, for heaven's sake! He's not as hot as the pictures."

"Aw, boo. That sucks."

Holly snickered. "He's hotter, Mel. Seriously, unbelievably, gorgeously *hot*. If he were anybody else, oh lord, I might just be tempted into misbehaving very badly…"

As if she'd misbehaved badly in forever. Her love life had been non-existent lately. Her last date hadn't gone so well. Mel had set her up with an attorney who'd spent most of the date on his phone and then interrogated her like she was one of his clients. In short, it'd been a long time since she'd had sex—and Ross made her think about it more than she should.

"So misbehave! Who cares? Does he seem interested in you?"

"I doubt it," she said truthfully. "I mean he's flirtatious, but I think he's that way naturally."

"He took you out for two meals. He didn't have to do that."

"No, but the Jeep's dead. He took me to dinner because I didn't have a way home."

"That doesn't explain breakfast. Also, he's rich—he's heard of Uber. Which means he wanted to take you to dinner and breakfast instead of letting you call for a ride."

Holly sighed. "Maybe so. But it doesn't change the fact he's a Blackthorne. They own this place—and I am not about to jeopardize my job by getting involved with one of the heirs to the throne. Especially one who soaks scantily clad women in champagne when he wins a race."

She had her sister to think of. If Emily needed something and insurance didn't cover it, Holly would have to come up with the money, which was why she socked away as much as she could. Oh, she could call Ricky—and she would—but her brother had never been super reliable with that kind of thing. He'd promise to pay her back. And then he'd conveniently forget. Uncle Evan and Aunt Brenda would help, but Holly didn't like to ask them. She wanted them to have a nice retirement, and since they were getting closer to that day all the time, she didn't want them raiding their 401k for her and Emily.

"Okay, so I understand not wanting to lose your job. Totally. But you aren't unemployable, Holly. You're a Brooks! A third generation whisky maker. There's any number of distilleries who'd snap you up if they could. And I'm not saying that because I think you need to bang Ross Blackthorne—though I totally do. I'm saying it because I don't want you thinking that's the only job you can get. You'd be an asset to any distillery."

"I know. But I don't want to leave Uncle Evan, or this place where I've worked since I left college."

She was certainly employable. But at what cost? She

hated to think about starting over somewhere else. Everything about Blackthorne Kentucky was new and state of the art, though they'd incorporated the old stillhouse into the design. Blackthorne wasn't Brooks Creek. It was bigger and better.

But it was all that was left of Brooks Creek, and that meant she wanted to stay right here. Besides, she got paid fairly well. If she went somewhere else, she might have to start at a lower salary.

"Do you really think Ross Blackthorne would hold it against you if you dated him and it didn't work out?"

"I don't know. I'm not sure I want to risk it. But Mel, we're speculating here, because it doesn't mean he's interested."

Mel snorted. "Honey, I'm not even there and I know he's interested. You're gorgeous and fun, and he's taken you out to eat twice. He didn't have to do that. Even if he was just being nice, he could have dropped you off without the meal last night. And this morning? He could have let you take that Uber in and not thought twice about it."

"You're hopelessly romantic, you know that? Ross Blackthorne is *not* interested in me. He's a nice guy, that's all. Do you know he lets kids sit in his two million dollar car and takes pictures of them? And he rolls down his window to talk to people who want to talk to him?"

"Makes sense. He's a racecar driver. He must like the attention."

"I thought that too—but it's more than that. He feels like he needs to give back. It's admirable."

"So you admire him?"

Holly frowned as she considered it. But she couldn't deny the truth. "Yeah, I think I do. A little bit anyway. I mean he's been nice to me even though I was curt with him all week."

"Nothing wrong with admiring him."

"Yeah, but I didn't want to admire him. I didn't even want to like him!"

"Do you like him?"

Holly dropped her forehead to her palm. "Unfortunately. I was all set to dislike him for being spoiled and rich, not to mention getting in my way, but he's kinda hard to dislike."

"That's not a big deal, Holly. So you like him. It's okay."

"It would be easier not to. I mean there's still the champagne thing, right?"

Mel made a noise. "Okay, look here, missy. I was calling in the first place to see if you wanted to go to the Boot tonight. Do a little dancing, a little flirting. Let down our hair. Amy and Becca are going. And I really think you need it now that I've heard all this. Ross Blackthorne is there being all sexy and admirable and you like him but you don't want to, right?"

"Pretty much."

"Then you need to come to the Boot and have a good time."

"I don't know, Mel…"

"Oh come on. It's ladies' night. And it's a three-day weekend for you. What do you have to lose?"

Holly thought about it. She liked to dance, and she liked going out with her friends. They got dressed up, went to dinner, and had a good time. It was a way to let off steam—and a way to meet men. Not that she'd met any men on those outings worth spending time with, but you never knew. Couldn't meet people if you didn't go out.

Besides, it was a good way to get Ross off her mind. Get herself back to reality.

"Okay, fine. I'll go."

IT WAS NEARING five p.m. when Ross knocked on Holly's open office door. She looked up from her computer. He'd hoped for a smile, but he didn't get one. "Yes?" she asked.

"It's almost five. Thought I'd go down and get to work on your Jeep."

"Oh. Right. How long will it take, do you think?"

"About twenty minutes or so with the right tools. Which I have." He'd tossed his toolbox in the truck this morning, knowing he'd need different sized wrenches and screwdrivers for the job.

"That's all?"

"Yep."

"And they wanted to charge me three hundred bucks?"

"That's right."

"Wow." She shook her head. "You never told me how much the starter was. I'd like to pay you for it."

"Receipt's in the truck. Can I get your keys?"

She reached into her purse and dug out her keys. He walked over to take them from her, but she stood and came around the desk, head down so that they nearly collided. He could have avoided it, but he didn't. Instead, he put his hands on her arms to steady her as she took a quick step back and stumbled.

Her head tilted so she could look up at him. He didn't let her go. His chest tightened. Her eyes were extraordinary. Blue-gray with little flecks of black. And the look she gave him didn't say *get away*.

Still, he eased his grip on her arms. "Careful."

"I, uh, yes," she replied. "I wasn't paying attention. Sorry."

"I'm not. Sorry that is."

She blinked as if she didn't quite know what to say. He

dropped his hands from her arms. Curled his fingers into the hand holding the keys and took them from her. His skin was electric where it brushed hers. Her breath hitched in. He thought she bit the inside of her lip based on the little dimple that appeared.

Heat curled into him, spreading through his body. His groin started to ache with need. Too much more and he'd be dipping his head to hers, tasting her sweet lips. He took a step back before he could do anything so foolish.

Foolish for right now, not forever. Foolish for where they were. Another time, another circumstance, and he'd definitely make the move.

"I'll just, uh, go down and change your starter."

"Yes. Thank you. I appreciate it. I'll owe you one."

"One what?" he asked, trying to interject humor into the moment.

"I don't know. A favor that only takes twenty minutes?"

Ross wanted to groan. He could immediately think of something that could take twenty minutes. Her mouth on his cock, for instance. Instead, he kept a straight face. "I'm sure I can think of something."

He didn't make it sound dirty, but he saw the instant her mind went there. The color spreading over her cheeks made it very apparent what she'd been thinking. "Okay, um, good," she said. "Just let me know."

"I definitely will." He grinned.

She waved her hand vaguely behind her. "I have to finish this report."

He took a couple of steps backward, toward the door, flipping her keys around his finger. "I'll meet you outside. Or I'll bring your keys back in if you aren't finished by then."

She stepped behind her desk as if needing it to shield her. "Thanks again."

"It's my pleasure," he told her, infusing the words with as much heat as he could. Then he turned and walked away, leaving her to dig herself out from under the weight of her embarrassment.

———

WHAT WAS the matter with her? Holly put her hands on her cheeks, feeling the heat glowing there. Was she really that awkward that she couldn't help but think dirty thoughts whenever Ross said something to her about favors and owing him?

Or was it just that he was too damned sexy and her mind was going to go there no matter what? Holly flopped into her chair and stabbed at her keyboard. Seriously, it had only been a matter of days since she'd looked at pictures of him surrounded by women making googly eyes and said no way in hell would she behave like that. Yet here she was, blushing and stammering and enjoying it entirely too much when he touched her.

She should have stepped away immediately when she'd nearly collided with him. But he'd put his hands on her to steady her, gazed into her eyes, and she'd been mesmerized. She'd even thought, for one brief second, that he might kiss her.

Holly closed her eyes. Because, dammit, she'd *wanted* him to do it. If he'd kissed her, she would have melted into him like she had no bones. Like she needed him to hold her up.

Argh!

Good thing Mel had called and convinced her to go to the Boot tonight. She really, *really*, needed to get dressed up and go have some fun. Too many hours at the distillery lately while she worked on the flavored product lines and tried to convince her uncle—who then had to convince the Blackthornes—why they needed to branch out and offer those beverages.

Holly finished up the document she was working on, closed it out, and gathered her things. It was ten after five and she needed to get downstairs and pray her Jeep was fixed, then head home and dig into her closet for the perfect outfit. She was already feeling excited about the outing, which told her that she desperately needed it. If she was lucky, maybe she'd meet some nice guy who'd ask her out and then she could put the idea of Ross Blackthorne and his sexy smile behind her for good.

He might be nice, but he was from a different world. A world he'd go back to just as soon as he got the chance.

Holly emerged into the bright sunlight of the employee parking lot. She could hear people laughing in front of the welcome center, which meant the last tour group was leaving the distillery. They ran tours all day from open to close, and they held tastings as well. Since the distillery had reopened under the Blackthorne name, the tours were jammed on most days—they'd even built a new welcome center to house the tourists as they arrived.

Holly's gaze went to her Jeep, and to the man bent over the engine. He'd removed his button-down shirt and only wore a white T-shirt now. A shirt that clung to muscles she'd only seen on the internet. But Ross Blackthorne really did have a defined back and shoulders, and his skin glistened with sweat. No wonder since the temperature today was in the nineties. The spot where she'd parked was shaded now, but it was still hot.

Ross looked up as she approached. His grin speared right into her, all the way down to her feminine center.

Hello, handsome!

84

"Just in time," he said. "You can start it up, see if I did it right."

She had no doubt he'd done it right. Or that he could do a lot of things right. Things she most definitely had *no* intention of pursuing.

Holly got inside and turned the key. The Jeep cranked to life, rumbling familiarly. Relief swept through her at the sound. She'd only been without her car for a day, but she'd felt stuck not being able to go where she wanted when she wanted. Sure, she could have taken an Uber—but it wasn't quite the same.

"Thank you," she said as he dropped a wrench into his toolbox and straightened. His white T-shirt had a couple of grease stains on it. It was also mostly wet and clung to his body like a second skin.

"No problem. Happy to do it."

"I, uh…" She had to drag her gaze from the way the T-shirt clung to his abs. And then she couldn't do a single thing but stare as he picked up the hem of his shirt and dragged it up his body. He wiped his face with the hem.

But instead of dropping it, he pulled the shirt off entirely—exposing a broad chest, tight muscles, and abs that looked like you could break a board across them.

Oh holy hell, he was beautiful…

Chapter 8

Ross wiped the shirt across his face and then tossed it
through the open window of his truck that sat parked
beside her Jeep. "You okay?" he asked.

Holly swallowed. Her throat was as dry as a desert.
"Of course. I'm just so happy that you fixed it. How much
do I owe you?"

She turned to her purse, needing something to do to
take her mind off the inevitable path it was starting to skip
down—Ross Blackthorne removing his jeans, sliding them
down his hips...

What kind of underwear would a hot racecar driver
wear? Boxers? Briefs? Boxer briefs? She hoped for the last
option—there was something seriously yummy about a
man in tight little shorts that showed every bulge.

"You don't owe me for the labor. And I thought I had
the receipt but I must have left it at home. I'll let you
know."

Holly dug out some bills because she was on autopilot
as she tried to reset her brain. She turned and thrust them
toward Ross. He dropped his gaze to her hand. Slowly slid

it back up to her eyes. He saw too deeply into her, she was sure, and she looked away. Cleared her throat. "Here's fifty bucks. I'll pay you the rest when you let me know the total."

"Not taking your money, Holly. Keep it."

She swung her gaze back to his. "What? But you said…"

"I know what I said. Not taking it though."

She wadded up the money. Clenched it in her fist as confusion rolled through her. "Not taking it now, or ever?"

His dark eyes glittered with heat. "What do you think?"

It hit her then. "I think you don't intend to take the money at all. You didn't leave the receipt at home. You know exactly how much the starter cost you, but you aren't going to tell me."

He smiled. "Bingo."

Holly gripped the steering wheel with one hand, held her closed fist in her lap. She couldn't drive away because the hood was still propped open. And her door was open too because she'd only jumped inside to start it up. Ross stood in the opening, so close she could smell him. He smelled like oil and sweat and whisky—and it was somehow the most delicious combination she'd ever smelled in her life. It made her tingle inside.

"That wasn't the deal," she said, trying to sound angry instead of aroused.

He shrugged. Put his hand on the support post. Lifted a leg and propped his foot on the running board. "I know. Consider it a thanks for teaching me how to run the distillery."

"I get paid for that. Every day."

"Yeah, but it's not part of your job description. You only got stuck with me because I wrecked a car and my dad is having a senior life crisis or something. So let me do the things I can do and then I'll feel like we're at least somewhat even."

She scowled. "I can afford to pay for the starter. If I gave the impression I couldn't, then I'm sorry. I'm not broke and I don't need your money, Mr. Blackthorne."

"Hey, hey, hey. What's with the mister?" He reached out and put a finger under her chin. Tipped her head in his direction. "Are you going to be pissed at me if I don't take your money? I didn't do it because I think you can't afford it—I did it because I wanted to. Just like letting those kids sit in my car. I *want* to and it makes me feel good that I made them happy. I want to make you happy, too."

Holly bit her lip and looked down. Away from his naked chest and the seriousness in those dark eyes. Away from the fullness of his mouth and the way she was really starting to ache to taste him. He wanted to make her happy? Oh, she could think of a few ways right now.

"I just don't want to give you the impression I'm a charity case."

"I don't have that impression at all. Look, if it makes you feel better, donate the money to the employee birthday fund or something. I don't feel right taking it."

She didn't like that he wouldn't let her pay him, but she also understood. And this was a compromise she could live with. She stuffed the money into her purse. "Okay, I will."

He sighed. "Okay, good."

He knotted her up inside. Twisted her into a pretzel. "I really do appreciate you fixing it for me. It's a weight off my mind for sure. If you hadn't—well, who knows where it might have stranded me?"

"Now you don't have to find out. That starter should last you a few years." He didn't move away from her door. His eyes were still hot on hers. "You promised to come to my garage, you know."

Her blood felt thick in her veins. "I know."

"What are you doing right now?"

"I-I can't. I'm going out with friends tonight."

He dropped his foot to the ground. Took his hand off the support. "Okay. Maybe sometime this weekend then."

She swallowed, suddenly wishing she hadn't agreed to go to the Boot at all. Because she could think of nothing better than going wherever Ross Blackthorne wanted to take her. But it was too late. He was already disengaging. "Um, sure. Sounds good."

"I'll text you."

He bent to pick up his toolbox, hefted it into his truck, then came over and put her hood down. She pulled her door closed and buckled her seatbelt. He walked over and put his hand on her windowsill. Sweat glistened on his chest. She imagined him stepping into the shower, water sluicing over his body, down that hard chest, over his abs, his groin…

"Uh, Holly?"

"What? Yes? You said something?"

He snorted. "I asked where you were going tonight."

"Oh, um, Mel likes to go to a place called Boot and Scoot. It's a honky-tonk bar. Country music, dancing. Known locally as the Boot."

She was babbling.

"Mel, huh? Thought you didn't have a boyfriend."

"Mel is a she, and she's my best friend." Holly paused. "Why are you asking?"

"Just wondering who or what is more appealing than me."

She gaped at him for a second. This was firmer ground. Ground she could stand on.

"Attention shoppers," she said in her best parody of an announcer voice. "Ego alert on aisle seven."

Ross laughed. He spread his hands and his muscles flexed—which meant he probably did it on purpose. She wasn't putting anything past him at the moment.

"How can you say no to a sweaty, sticky dude who smells like grease? You have no taste, Holly Brooks."

"I have plenty of taste. And you have plenty of ego."

He grinned. "Then we balance each other out, don't we?" He backed away from her, turned and opened the driver's door on his truck. "Have fun tonight. And don't accept any drinks from strangers."

"I wouldn't even think of it."

"Good." He got in and started his truck. A slight breeze rolled through the parking lot, ruffling his hair through the open window as he turned to look at her. "See you later, Holly."

"See you," she said.

His face disappeared behind the dark tint as he powered the window up. Holly put her Jeep in gear and drove toward the highway. Ross was right behind her. He stayed there until she made the turn for home, and then he was gone.

It shouldn't disappoint her that she was going out with Mel instead of spending time with Ross Blackthorne. But it did.

ROSS SWUNG by the team garage on the way home. He wasn't sure they'd still be there with the race in Chicago this weekend and qualifying starting tomorrow, but as luck would have it they were getting ready to pull out. His car sat inside the hauler. The hauler was closed, but Ross knew what he'd see if he opened the door. The black exterior panels were all shiny and sleek, and the Blackthorne barrel and thistle logo was emblazoned on the roof, broadcasting to millions of viewers that it was a whisky worth choosing.

The engine would be tuned to perfection, the suspension would be stiff and the tires sticky. He could almost taste the asphalt in his mouth, feel the road beneath him as the car burned up the pavement. The steering wheel would vibrate with power beneath his hands, and his spotter would be talking in his ear as he navigated the pack.

Except it wouldn't because he wasn't going.

A current of resentment flooded him. Sometimes he hated that Blackthorne logo and the control it exerted over his life. Not the logo precisely, but what it stood for.

Pride. Tradition. Legacy.

Sacrifice.

Bitterness twisted in his gut as he pictured his father back in Boston, meddling in his life without knowing or caring what it cost him. But then Ross thought of Holly Brooks and how hard she worked to make everything run smoothly at the distillery. Of how hard she'd worked to teach him how to be an executive vice president of his own family's company

Was that guilt following on the heels of his anger?

Yeah, it was. Because it wasn't Holly's fault he was pissed at his father. It wasn't her fault that being a Blackthorne affected his life in ways he couldn't control and she'd ended up saddled with him.

Ross kept hoping Brock would call and tell him that he'd talked Graham Blackthorne into letting Ross drive again, but he knew that wasn't going to happen anytime soon. Dad was angry and hurt and lashing out like a wounded lion. Rather than admit what was going on between him and Mom, rather than do something to fix it, he'd rather sit on high in Boston and make Ross's life hell.

But is it hell? Really?

The look on Holly's face as he'd taken his off shirt flashed through his mind. If they'd been alone somewhere…

Ross shoved a hand through his hair. Hell, he did *not* need to be thinking about that.

So okay, maybe his life wasn't precisely hell right now. But working at the distillery definitely wasn't what he wanted to be doing.

Several of his team members realized he was in the garage. They came over and started talking excitedly about the car and what they were going to do in Chicago this weekend. But nobody brought up the possibility of him driving. They knew he wasn't going to. It made his chest tight with anger and frustration, but there was nothing he could do.

Martin Temple emerged from his office and everyone scattered. He was a wiry, gray-haired son of a bitch who took no shit from anyone. He was also the best damned performance guy in the business. He could eke out another few horsepower from any engine, given enough time.

"Hey, Ross. Didn't expect to see you today."

Ross shook the hand Martin offered. "Didn't expect to swing by. But I had some time, so here I am. Everything going well with the test drives?"

Martin had said so on the phone, but Ross wanted to see his face when he said it.

The other man nodded. "Oh yeah. Eric's got the hang of her. He'll be fine."

"When are you pulling out?"

"In about twenty minutes."

"It's a little late, isn't it?"

Martin shrugged. "We've got time. Didn't want to get there too early. Too many questions going to come our way when you don't show."

Ross folded his arms over his chest. He'd put the Oxford back on, but he could still smell the oil and grease from Holly's Jeep. And now the odor of tires and oil and gas in the garage. Smells he loved.

"Yeah, well, I'm working on it. My dad will come to his senses soon enough. Blackthorne has too much money invested in this team to leave the driving to somebody else."

And Ross had too much invested in his own success to let it all go. The future of his motorsport company depended on it.

Martin's bushy brows drew down. "Eric's a fine driver, Ross. You know that. You trained him, and he's qualified for the series."

"Yeah, I know."

"He'll be fine."

"Yep. Where is he?"

"Went ahead of us. He wanted to get to the hotel, get settled in."

"I'll be cheering for you on Sunday. I want the team to win —regardless of whether or not I'm the one in the driver's seat."

Martin squeezed his shoulder. "I know you do. You're a fine driver, Ross. One of the best. Your daddy will realize it soon enough. Until he does, we've got no choice but to go ahead without you."

"It's fine. I'll see you next week."

"You could fly up if you wanted. Join us in pit lane."

He could. All he had to do was charter a plane for the short flight. But he didn't think he wanted to be there with the grit and the noise and the excitement—and *not* be the one driving. Not this time.

"I might do that."

Ross left the garage and climbed into his truck. Then

he went home and entered the big house he'd bought when he'd started spending the season in Kentucky. He hadn't noticed how lonely it was before. But now he walked across the spotless kitchen with its gleaming stainless appliances, its high-gloss cabinets and marble counters, and he heard the echo of his feet on the terrazzo floors.

The living room was also big. Also empty. He'd hired an interior designer and given her carte blanche. She'd given him a modern space with clean lines and open spaces that felt, well, empty. Not that he'd noticed it before, but now that he'd been inside Holly's quaint little cottage, he couldn't help but think of the small rooms with warm furniture and bright, breezy fabrics. And all he'd seen had been her hallway and living room. He wondered what her kitchen looked like. Her bedroom.

He imagined a lot of flowery fabric and antiques for some reason. Pink. Lots of pink.

"Shit."

He had to stop thinking about Holly Brooks's bedroom. In fact, he had to stop thinking about Holly Brooks. He knew he shouldn't go there with her. She was supposed to be off limits because she was a company employee.

And yet he wanted to. More than he'd wanted anything in a long time. Was it because he couldn't race right now? Did he see her as a different kind of challenge, one that could take his mind off of racing for a while?

Ross stalked into his bedroom, shed his clothes on the floor, and headed for the giant walk-in shower that had no glass walls, no shower curtains. He flipped on the water, knowing it would be instantly hot—though it was probably cold water he needed when he again thought about how Holly looked at him when he'd peeled off his shirt.

Like she could eat him up. Like she hadn't had a man

in a very long time and she was dying of need. Not that she'd let him see that look for long. She'd quickly masked it.

Hell, maybe he'd imagined it.

But what if he hadn't? Holly was headed for a bar tonight. With friends, sure, but what if she met some guy and looked at him like that? And what if that guy pressed her, took advantage of her?

Ross growled. He couldn't let it happen. He didn't want it to happen.

He knew it was a flimsy excuse for what he was about to do, but hell, it was enough of one.

He finished the shower in record time and walked into his closet, looking up and down the rows of clothing stacked one over the other. He had custom suits and T-shirts and khakis and holey jeans and—ah yes, cowboy boots.

Just what he needed for a honky-tonk bar.

Chapter 9

Holly leaned back in her chair and took a sip of her Whisky Sour, made with Blackthorne bourbon, of course, while Amy and Becca flirted with a couple of guys in cowboy hats who'd stopped by their table. Mel was currently dancing with a guy she had the hots for who'd showed up tonight unexpectedly.

Holly twirled the stirrer in her drink and let her gaze slide across the bar. It was crowded tonight, but it always was for a ladies' night. The music was loud and the food and drinks were reasonable and plentiful. A basket of fries sat on the table, half-eaten, along with a plate of nachos. Holly scooped one of the chips up and popped it into her mouth.

"Hey, baby," a voice said, and she glanced up at a guy who smiled down at her, beer bottle in hand, plaid shirt open to a white T-shirt underneath. Of course he had on a cowboy hat. She liked cowboy hats—and this guy didn't look bad at all.

"Hey, there," she said, ignoring that he'd called her baby for the moment.

He dragged out Mel's chair. "You look lonely. Mind if I join you?"

Annoyance skated at the edges of her awareness. But maybe she was just on edge after those couple of episodes with Ross today. Had he held onto her on purpose in her office when she'd nearly plowed into him? And what about his shirt and the invitation to see his garage? What did that mean?

"It's a free country," she said to the guy as he plopped down beside her.

"Yeah, woohoo, sure is!" He tipped the beer back and drained half of it.

Holly wondered how many beers he'd had and whether or not it was time to make her excuses to her friends and go home. They'd been here for an hour already. Surely that was enough time. She'd hoped she'd be more into it than she was tonight, but all she wanted was to be home where it was quiet.

"What's your name, doll?" the guy asked.

Holly smiled tightly. "Well it's not doll. Or baby. Or honey."

He made a face. One of those faces that said he was surprised and insulted at the same time. *Hoo boy, here we go.*

"You one of them femi-nazis or something?"

"You mean a feminist? Yeah, I guess I am." Asshat. What made men like him think they had the right to act like jerks whenever a woman wanted a little respect? "Maybe this was a bad idea and you need to move on to another table."

He took another slug of beer. "Nope, I don't think so. I like a feisty girl. Makes it more fun."

"Makes what more fun? Getting rejected?"

He threw a look over his shoulder. Probably at his buddies who'd no doubt bet him to come over here and pick her up. When he looked at her again, his eyes were meaner than before. "You've got quite a mouth, you know that?"

Anger started to bubble in her veins. "You've got quite a mouth too, sugar. You started out nice but then you had to call me doll. And the insults haven't stopped since. I'm thinking we aren't going to work out, baby cakes. So maybe head back over to your friends and try again with someone else."

Amy threw a look in Holly's direction, but the music was too loud for her to hear what was being said. Still, she nudged Becca. The guys they'd been talking to had gone to the bar, presumably for more drinks. Holly gave them a look. They both rose and came to her side.

Asshat looked at the three of them, his expression mean. Then he put the beer down and stood, grabbing Holly's arm, his fingers digging in deep as he dragged her up. Amy and Becca lunged for her, but he started dragging her toward the rear of the bar, his strength too much for them to stop him. There was a door back there that led outside. People often went out to smoke, or to talk where they could be heard. Holly jerked against his hold but she couldn't break free. Not yet anyway.

And the bar was too crowded for anyone to realize that what was going on was more than a disagreement between a couple. Amy and Becca were following, yelling at them, but even that looked like a couple of girls angry with their friend's boyfriend. Holly cast wildly around for someone she knew, someone who would know that she had no idea who this guy was—but she didn't see anybody.

He'd reached the door and slapped it open when a hand closed over Holly's shoulder. She didn't know who'd come to her rescue and she didn't care so long as he got her away from this guy. Somehow, he detached Asshat's hand from her arm, and then he was between her and the other guy.

She stood behind the man who'd intervened, shaking with fear and fury both. And then he lunged forward, shoving Asshat out the door. Amy and Becca caught up to her at that moment.

"Oh my God, who is that?" Amy asked. "He got here just in time."

"I don't know," Holly said, but she pushed her way forward, through the door to where the two men squared off. Her savior's back was to her. He wore a dark shirt, black or blue maybe, faded jeans, and cowboy boots. Asshat was busy yelling something. And then his entire demeanor changed and his eyes widened. He swayed in place, clearly drunk.

"Ross Blackthorne? Holy shit, man, I effing love the way you drive. And that wreck—bad break. Sorry 'bout that."

Holly gaped at the two of them. "Ross?" she called out.

He glanced at her, his eyes flashing fire. "Let me take care of this. Go back inside."

Her heart started to race. He was here. Now. And he'd saved her from that drunken asshole. "Don't hit him. He's not worth it."

Asshat's gaze slid to her. "She your girl, Ross?"

"Yeah, she's my girl."

Holly's heart tripped and then sped up. Amy gasped. Becca just said, "Oh my. You got some 'splainin' to do, girl."

Asshat held up both hands. "Man, I didn't know. I'd have never touched her if I did."

Ross growled, fists clenching at his sides. "What you don't seem to understand is that you shouldn't touch *any* woman without her permission. Ever."

"She was mouthy. I didn't mean nothing."

Ross took a menacing step forward. "Dude, I don't know who you are, but I'm going to find out. And when I do, I'll make life harder on you than you ever thought possible—unless you apologize to the lady and then go away and never come back. I hear you even step foot in this place, I'll find you. You don't want me to find you."

Asshat turned to her, a completely different expression on his face. It wasn't meanness this time, but fear. Fear of his idol.

Geez, the power these race drivers had over their fans. She'd had no idea until she'd met him. Because she didn't watch NASCAR. Didn't understand it. But when people loved the sport, they really loved it.

"I, um, I'm sorry, miss. So sorry. I swear I'm sorry. It'll never happen again. Swear."

"All right," Ross said. "Now get out of my sight."

The guy's buddies had come outside at some point and were gaping at Ross. Clearly, they recognized him too. Her heart skipped for a second as she envisioned one of them taking a swing at him—because there were bound to be some guys for whom fighting a famous driver would be a crowning achievement, but fortunately neither of them seemed inclined. They grabbed their buddy and herded him toward the parking lot while he kept hollering how sorry he was.

Ross stalked over to her. Put his hands on her arms. "You okay, Holly?"

He smelled so good. Like spice and soap and, yes, even whisky. Blackthorne whisky. Not like he'd been drinking it, but like it was a part of him. She supposed it probably was in a way.

"I'm fine." She pulled in a breath. "I'm really happy to see you, Ross."

His fierce expression didn't ease. "What happened?"

"He sat down at my table. And then he called me doll and babe, which you know I don't like."

Ross didn't look any less angry, but he snorted for a brief second. "Yeah, I know that."

"Well, he didn't like it when I called him out on it. Then he started to drag me outside."

"Hey, man—are you really Ross Blackthorne?"

Holly jerked her gaze toward a man who'd approached them. He practically bounced from foot to foot in his excitement.

For the first time since she'd met him, Holly saw Ross struggling with his tendency to be accommodating to his fans. The fact he struggled *because* of her wasn't lost on her. He wanted to protect her, make sure she was okay. He didn't want to answer fan questions or be social. He wanted to focus on her.

It melted her heart in ways she didn't understand. She put a light hand on his chest, felt his warmth seeping into her skin. Smiled shakily, because it's all she had. "It's okay. I'm okay. Talk to your fans."

"I don't want to," he said, his voice low and angry. "I want to get you out of here."

"Sign his ball cap or whatever. Then I'll go with you."

Because she wanted out of there as much as he wanted to take her. But more than that, she wanted to go with him specifically. She'd thought she'd get to the Boot tonight and meet a guy she might want to see again. She realized now that what she really wanted was to spend time with Ross Blackthorne.

Oh God, she was so screwed. He was all wrong for her —and he wasn't the kind of guy who stayed with one woman. She knew that. But maybe being with him was like driving a racecar. The thrill of the ride might be worth the regret once it was over.

Ross closed his eyes for a second. She saw pain in his expression. Pain and sorrow and even, surprisingly, uncertainty. About what?

But then he opened his eyes and gave her arms a squeeze before turning to meet the gaze of the man who still stood hopefully by. He held out his hand and the guy took it enthusiastically.

"Yeah, buddy, I'm Ross. How are you?"

———

ROSS DIDN'T KNOW if she'd still be there when he was done talking to the group of guys who crowded outside to discuss the race in which he'd flamed out—plus his other races this season—but when he finally managed to excuse himself and turn, she was there. Leaning against the wall, looking beautiful with her lustrous red hair and sparkling eyes. She wore a pale blue dress with buttons down the center and cowboy boots that had a bit of glitter. And she smiled softly when their eyes met.

There were three women with her, which he didn't notice until he took a step toward her and they all crowded in close as if protecting her. Inside, the music thumped and people hollered, but outside it was marginally quieter. At least enough so that you could have a conversation.

"Girls, meet Ross Blackthorne," Holly said. "Ross, these are my friends—Amy, Becca, and Melissa, aka Mel."

He'd thought Mel was a guy when Holly'd mentioned the name earlier. Mel was definitely not a guy. Mel was tall and curvy and gorgeous. His usual type, from the top of her blonde head to the bottom of her long legs. Legs that went on for days.

He looked at her and felt... *nothing.* Absolutely nothing.

But when he looked at Holly? His insides lit up like a thousand fireflies whirled beneath his skin.

"Nice to meet you," he said to all three of them.

"What are your intentions with our girl here?" Mel asked.

Ross blinked. He would have laughed, but these ladies were serious. They stood close to Holly as if planning to do battle if he provoked them.

"My intentions are to get her out of here."

"And then what?"

"Hush, Mel," Holly said, her pretty skin flushing. It might be dark outside, but there was enough light that he could tell. And even if there wasn't, he was pretty sure he knew when Holly was blushing by now. He knew by the way her head tipped down, the way she tried to hide her cheeks behind a curtain of hair. The way she peered up at him beneath her lashes.

"Holly?" he asked.

She took a step toward him. Caught his hand when he held his out for her. God that felt right. Why did it feel right?

"I'm ready."

He tugged her into his side, slipped his arm around her body. It was the first time he'd been this close to her. Sparks snapped inside him in response.

"You sure about this, Hols?" Mel asked her friend.

"It's fine," Holly said. "I'm ready to get out of here. Y'all stay and have fun."

"Okay. But you hurt her, Ross Blackthorne, and I'll make sure you regret it," Mel called out as Ross and Holly started to walk away

"Mel," Holly groaned over her shoulder. "Enough."

Ross stopped and turned back to the tall blonde. "Holly is safe with me. I promise you."

Mel frowned and folded her arms over her chest. "You better be right about that."

"Bye, Mel," Holly said. "I'll call you tomorrow."

Mel didn't say anything else and nobody stopped them as they slipped between cars. Ross had an urge to grab Holly, turn her and push her against a parked car so he could kiss her.

But he held that urge in check because the first time he kissed Holly, it wouldn't be in the parking lot of a bar. She deserved better than that. He hadn't let go of her hand, and she hadn't tried to pull away. He led her to his truck, opened the passenger door, and helped her inside. She didn't protest that she could open her own door. He took that as a good sign.

He went around to his side and started the truck, the growl of the engine familiar and welcome in the midst of all these crazy feelings swirling inside him.

"What are you even doing here, Ross?"

He gripped the wheel with both hands, considering what to say. "I went by the garage. They had the car loaded in the hauler and they were getting ready to pull out. I should be going with them, but I'm not. So I went home—and it was so damned empty I didn't want to be there anymore."

"So you came looking for me? Or you just kind of happened to show up when I needed you most?"

And thank God he had. When he'd seen that guy with her, he'd known something was wrong. "You're the only person I know around here who's outside the racing world. Hell, you don't even give a shit about the racing world. And I guess I thought, if I could be with you, maybe I wouldn't feel so lonely tonight."

Not what he'd intended to say, but it was too late now. She was watching him with those pretty eyes, her brows drawing down into a frown as she studied him.

"Crazy, right?" he said when she didn't say anything. "You don't like me much. Or maybe that's precisely why I'm here. You don't bullshit me and you don't seem to want anything from me. You don't want a piece of me the way everyone else does."

She dropped her gaze from his, swallowed, and his dick started to harden. Because that single move told him everything he needed to know about what she wanted. She wanted *him*. And not because he was Ross Blackthorne—or at least he didn't think so. She wanted him because they had chemistry. Because something hot burned between them even though she'd been doing her best to ignore it.

From the minute she'd strode out of the distillery with her clipboard and told him where to park, until now, every interaction they'd had had been leading them to this.

"I don't want to like you," she said softly. "But I do."

Chapter 10

Oh God, she'd said it. She'd told him the truth. She liked him. There was no turning back from that. She thought he might grin or smirk or do any number of things that would make her roll her eyes in exasperation.

But he didn't. He looked at her with a solemn expression, his handsome face giving nothing away. "I like you too."

Her heart thumped. She wanted to ask what that meant. *Exactly* what that meant. But she couldn't say the words. How silly would it sound anyway?

"Thanks for saving me. I was planning to knee him in the nuts once we got outside and he stopped moving, but I'm glad it didn't come to that."

Ross's eyes widened a little. "Me too. Not because I care what happens to him, but because he might have hurt you before you got the chance."

Holly shivered. That had been a possibility, sure. "Do you really think he'll stay away from the Boot?"

"He will. If I have to buy the damned place and make a rule he doesn't get to enter. Ever."

His answer shocked her. He had the money. He could definitely do it. It wouldn't really happen but she was flattered anyway. "I don't even know who he is. I never saw him before."

"I do."

"You do?"

"Yes. The guys I was just talking to told me. I know his name and where he works. He won't ever bother you again, Holly. I wasn't kidding when I said that."

"Don't do anything crazy, Ross. It's not worth it." She was thinking of his career as a driver, and also of the Blackthorne family name. There was nothing he could do that wouldn't get broadcast to the world and dissected by the media. And she wasn't going to be the cause of his career or family suffering.

He frowned. "It's worth it to me. That man had no respect for you. He was angry that you stood up to him, and he planned to make you pay for it."

"I know. But it's over now. I just want to forget it. Can we go? Please?"

"Sure." He reversed onto the street, and then shoved the truck into gear. He squeezed the pedal and the vehicle leapt forward. "You want to go home?"

"No. Not yet." Because what if he dropped her off and that was it? She wasn't ready to say goodbye to him. As dangerous as it was, she wanted to spend more time together. Just a little more time.

"I didn't ask about your Jeep. Can you leave it overnight or do we need to get it later?"

Later. That implied he'd be with her for a while. "It's at home. Mel picked me up and we rode together."

"Good. So," he said as they drove through the darkness. "Where do you want to go?"

Holly leaned her head back on the seat. She felt a little

light-headed, but it wasn't from drinking. It was him. Being with him. Her heart sped recklessly while her brain tried to throw on the brakes.

Her heart wasn't listening. She said the first thing that popped into her head. "The distillery."

He glanced at her. "Really? Why?"

"Not the distillery, precisely. The house there."

"Was that your family house?"

"My grandparents lived there, then my mom and dad. I was born there, actually. I came too quickly. They couldn't even get out the door to the hospital."

"I'm sorry you had to sell it, then."

She shrugged. "It goes with the distillery. I believe the plan is to turn it into a restaurant and hotel."

"Does that bother you?"

"It used to. It doesn't anymore."

"Why not?"

"It needs a lot of work, and a lot of care. I used to think if I could buy it, I could fix it up. But I can't. And I don't want to, really. Living onsite twenty-four hours a day? No, that wouldn't be good. It wasn't good for my father. He was always working."

"I understand. The Blackthorne distillery is about a mile's walk from the estate, so it seemed like my dad was always headed there whenever we were in residence."

"In residence? You didn't live there full time?"

Ross shook his head. "No. The family summer home is in King Harbor, Maine. That's where the distillery is. But we lived in Boston during the year."

She shouldn't be surprised. The Blackthornes were loaded. Of course they didn't live and work near the distillery three hundred and sixty-five days a year. She couldn't imagine what that was like since her family had always lived on the grounds of their distillery.

"No wonder you aren't a whisky maker at heart. You didn't grow up around it every day of your life."

"I was around it enough, believe me. Dad liked to take us all there whenever we were in Maine. Wanted to give us an appreciation for our heritage." He made the turn toward the distillery. "Which I have. I just wasn't interested in actually working in the business. I have brothers and cousins who do, and who love it."

"How many of you are there?"

"Seven. All boys. No sisters. We were raised together when my aunt and uncle died in a plane crash."

Holly frowned. She remembered reading about a plane crash in which Graham Blackthorne's brother and his wife died. It had been during her research into the Blackthornes after Ricky and Uncle Evan accepted their offer to buy the Brooks Creek facilities.

"I'm sorry about your aunt and uncle. That must have been difficult."

"It was. They were great. I still miss them. Logan, Brock, and Phillip moved in with us right away. Mom did her best to make sure they felt at home with us."

"Brock... he's the head of marketing and brand management, right?"

"Yeah, that's him. Why, has he done something you don't like?" Ross asked with a laugh.

"No, not yet. He's very particular though." They often got directives from the head office, signed by Brock, which dictated a matter of marketing or policy regarding the Blackthorne name.

"Yeah, he is. The brand means a lot to him. To all of us, but he's the keeper and enforcer."

"I bet he wouldn't be happy if you'd punched that guy."

Ross pulled up to the abandoned house and stopped.

"No, he definitely wouldn't have been. Good thing I didn't."

"Good thing," she echoed.

"So, what did you want to see here?"

Holly pushed her door open. "I just wanted to see the house. I haven't come here in a few months now."

In the distance, the distillery was lit up with exterior lights that picked out the Blackthorne logo. She could smell the mash in the air. It was sweet and it made her heart glad.

Holly jumped down and shut the passenger door. Ross came around to her side and waited for her to decide what happened next. She walked toward the house, the gravel crunching beneath her feet. Behind her, she could hear Ross following. She stepped up onto the porch that ran the length of the house. It creaked beneath her weight.

Ross joined her. "Who has the keys? I'd love to see inside."

Holly grinned. "Ah, those would be in the office. But I have a spare."

"You do?"

She walked over to the letter box that perched beside the door. Then she reached inside and pulled a key from under the tape that held it against the front of the box. She smiled when she flourished it for him.

"Rebel," he said.

She handed him the key. "Sometimes. But the honor is yours, Mr. Blackthorne."

He frowned at her as if trying to decide if she was serious. Then he stuck the key in the lock and turned it. The door swung open with the kind of creak that typically graced haunted houses.

"After you."

She pushed the door open farther and stepped inside.

The house was much as they'd left it, with furniture and antiques that filled the rooms. They were covered in cloths, however. She knew what was under them, but Ross did not.

"Wow," he said. She knew what he saw. Detailed wood-work on the walls and doors. Tall windows with the orig-inal glass. Soaring ceilings and ornate fireplaces.

"They don't make houses like they used to." It was true. Today's tract houses lacked so much character. That was why she loved the old ones. Someone like Ross though —he could renovate an old beauty, or he could have a modern home built that contained all these features. She envied him having that kind of choice.

"My family home in King Harbor—it has these kinds of details. It's been renovated for modern comfort though."

"Nothing wrong with a new old house," she said.

"New old house?"

"You know, where they use old materials but build a new home."

"Ah, got it. That's not King Harbor though. It's old, and it's modern in places. The kitchen in particular."

"Can't have an ancient kitchen," she said as she started to walk across the living room.

But Ross caught her arm. Turned her toward him. She went willingly. When he tugged her into his arms, she didn't protest. It was as if she'd known. As if this was the right place and time.

"I've wanted to do this since I first laid eyes on you," he said.

She clung to him, clutching his arms as he tilted her head back. And then his mouth crashed down on hers—and the world started to spin.

SHE TASTED SWEET, like sugar and bourbon, and as her tongue met his, Ross thought for the barest of moments that his knees might buckle. Except he was stronger than that, and he'd kissed far too many women for one to affect him so strongly.

And yet she *was* affecting him. More than he'd like. Her tongue stroked tentatively against his and he fisted her dress in his hands, pulling her tighter to him. It wouldn't take long for her to know exactly how much she affected him if they stayed this close together. Already, he was growing hard—and no amount of control in the world was going to prevent it.

Holly slipped her arms around his neck, arched her body into his, her mouth opening wider beneath his own. They kissed for long minutes, lost in each other as their hearts hammered and their bodies responded to the heat between them.

She was pliant against him, her mouth warm and wonderful. He wanted to lose himself in her sweetness.

"Holly," he groaned as she moved against him, brushing his erection with her hips. Sending a shudder down his spine. "We have to stop."

She tipped her head back to look up at him. "But we just started."

He took a breath to steady himself. "I know. But I want a lot more than this kiss—and I don't think you're ready for it."

Her tongue darted over her lips and he nearly groaned again. But then she took a step backward, breaking the contact between them. "I'm sorry. I shouldn't have done that. You're my boss, and—"

He put a hand over her mouth, halting the words.

"First of all, you didn't do anything—I did. I kissed you. And I'm thrilled you kissed me back, by the way. I want more of that, but I also want to be in control of myself—which I barely am right now. Second, I'm not your boss."

Her eyes gleamed with heat as he peeled his hand away from her lips. She swayed a little on her feet.

Great, she was drunk. That explained a lot about her reactions tonight. Her guard was down or she'd be giving him hell instead of kissing him and making him crazy.

"You're a Blackthorne at the Blackthorne Kentucky distillery," she said softly. "You are most definitely the boss. Even if you don't know a new barrel from a used barrel, or ten year-old bourbon from recent harvest. You outrank us all, bossman."

He didn't want to be her boss. Not at the distillery anyway. In bed, however…

"I'm a Blackthorne, yes—but you're far more valuable to the distillery than I am, make no mistake. And as for that kiss—you're splitting hairs, Holly. You didn't kiss me. I kissed you. And I want to do it again. But I'd prefer to do it when you're sober. I want to know you're making the choice with all your wits about you."

Her eyebrows lifted. It was dark in the house, but a shaft of moonlight spilled through the windows and across the floor. It was just enough to see her.

"I'm not drunk. I was milking my drinks tonight. I had two, by the way. And yes, I know you kissed me first. But I didn't push you away. And I definitely kissed you back. I wanted to do it."

She turned and walked away from him, going over to run her hand across a cloth-covered table. He watched her progress through the room, her movements graceful and unhurried as she touched furniture and woodwork. Then she went over and opened a door that led onto the back porch running the length of the house.

Ross followed her outside, his dick still throbbing with arousal. Holly went over and sat down on a porch swing, rocking it gently. A pond sparkled in the moonlight a short distance away. Frogs croaked a night song and lightning bugs lit the darkness with their blinking yellow abdomens.

Feelings he didn't understand swirled inside him. He was out of his element here and he couldn't seem to get his equilibrium back. Like losing control on the track, he couldn't stop the spin.

"I used to sit out here at night when I was a kid," she finally said. "It was always so peaceful. I loved the sounds. And the smell of mash. Can you smell it?"

He didn't have to try very hard. "I do." He wasn't certain where she was going with this conversation, but he realized that he didn't care. He was happy just being here with her. If they sat on the swing all night and never said another word, he'd be content.

Well, maybe not content, he corrected. He wouldn't be content until he'd made love to her. That wasn't happening tonight, though. Maybe it shouldn't happen at all, but he knew himself well enough to know that he was going to ignore the voice that told him to be careful.

Careful wasn't what he did.

He went over and sat down beside her. She didn't try to move away from him. He pushed gently in rhythm with her as the swing rocked back and forth. Eventually, he put his hand along the back of the swing, twisted his fingers into a lock of her hair and twirled it.

So soft and silky. He lifted it to his nose, inhaled her shampoo. Vanilla and honey maybe. She didn't pull away at the intimate gesture.

"Thank you again for intervening tonight," she said

softly. "I couldn't seem to make anyone understand he was taking me outside against my will. It was crowded and I couldn't find anyone I knew. I tried to get away, but he was too strong." She sucked in a breath. "And then there you were, my savior."

Anger twisted deep inside again. "I'm not gonna lie—I wanted to tear that guy's head off. I should have." He hated that he'd heard both his cousin Brock and Martin Temple inside his brain, warning him not to get violent in a public place. The damage to the brand, to the racing team, blah blah blah.

"No, you shouldn't have. You did the right thing and you know it. You don't need some asshole suing Blackthorne Enterprises just because your family is loaded. The media would have a field day."

"They would."

"And I'd have been upset that I was the one who caused it to happen."

"No, he'd have been the one who caused it. Not you."

She lay her head back on the porch swing and gazed up at him. "You're sweet."

He scooted closer, cupped her cheek in his fingers. "I'm not sweet, Holly. I'm angry that someone thought they could touch you without repercussions. I'm angry that I couldn't do more than I did. That I had to think of the damned brand instead of what you deserved."

She put her fingers over his lips. His mouth tingled at her touch. A fierce possessiveness leapt inside him.

"You did exactly what you're supposed to do," she said. "I wouldn't have wanted you to do anything differently."

"I want to kiss you again," he told her when she pulled her fingers away.

Her lashes dipped to her cheeks. "I want that too," she whispered.

Chapter 11

This was insanity. Sheer insanity. But sitting here on the porch swing with Ross, talking to him, she wanted to try that kiss again.

Because the first one had been pretty damned spectacular. It wasn't just that she hadn't been kissed in a long time. She might not have been, but she could still tell a great kiss from a mediocre one.

Some guys kissed you and all you wanted was for it to end. Too much tongue, mouths open too wide, a general icky feeling that you knew would only stop when the kiss stopped.

And then there were the ones who kissed nicely. Just enough tongue, soft mouths, attuned to how you were feeling about the whole thing.

Then there was Ross. He tugged her toward him on the swing. She went willingly. Even when he reached down and picked up her legs, turning her so she was draped across his lap, she went with the flow. Her nerve endings sizzled with anticipation. He looped an arm around her for support, tipped her head back with his fingers on her chin.

He didn't immediately kiss her though. He seemed to be studying her, and she started to squirm. What if he found her lacking somehow? What if he came to his senses and decided that kissing her was too complicated?

Because it was complicated. Not only was she nothing like the women he usually kissed, he was also a Blackthorne and she was a Blackthorne employee. Sure, he didn't intend to be at the distillery for long—but what if he was? What if he never went back to driving and he was suddenly there all the time, running the show? He'd have the power over who got the master distiller job some day—and it wouldn't be her if things went bad between them.

And yet that still wasn't enough to make her stop him. His head descended and her eyes closed automatically, her heart hammering a staccato beat in her chest. Ross's lips touched hers, skimming lightly over them. Torturing her.

"You taste so sweet, Holly," he whispered.

She looped her arms around his neck, tugging him down. "Stop teasing me, Ross. Kiss me."

He chuckled. "Haven't you heard that saying about anticipation making it sweeter?"

"Probably. But it's bullshit. At least in this case."

He laughed outright. "God, you're cute." Then he slanted his mouth over hers and kissed her like she'd been wanting him to do.

Their tongues tangled, and heat spread through her body. It centered on her sex, making her wet and achy and desperate. Ross was careful not to move his hands anywhere personal—but she wanted him to. Badly.

She touched his face, slid her fingers into his hair, and kissed him back with all the passion she possessed. It was risky and crazy and joyful and she couldn't seem to make herself think of it as a danger to her heart.

He skimmed his fingers down her throat—and then he

cupped her breast and she thought she might die.

He hesitated, as if waiting for her to stop him, but she didn't. And then he grew bolder, rubbing his thumb back and forth over her nipple while she gasped from the sensations streaking through her.

She could feel him beneath her thighs where they lay across his lap. He was hard. Ready. For *her*. It made her shudder deep inside. Need flared hot and heavy. Her body grew achy. Her sex actually hurt from how aroused he made her.

And then he stopped. Just like that, he lifted his head and removed his hand and the kiss was over. A dull throbbing echoed inside her. Disappointment and uncertainty twined together as embarrassment threatened to overrule the whole thing.

"I can't keep doing this," he said, his voice more gravelly than before. Hoarse. "I want you, Holly. But not on a porch swing in the dark. I want to strip you slowly, kiss my way over every inch of your body, and then I want to lay you down on a soft bed and make you come for me again and again."

Holly gulped. She shouldn't want any of that with him, but she did. So badly. "Take me home, Ross. It's not that far away…"

He kissed her forehead. Sighed. "I'm going to take you home. But I'm not coming inside with you. I've told you what I want, but I want you to make sure it's what you want too."

He helped her stand, his hand firmly clasped around hers as he sat on the porch swing and looked up at her. "You're so beautiful, Holly. You make me feel things I don't understand."

She put her hand over his mouth. "Don't say things like that, Ross. You don't have to in order to convince me to sleep with you. I'm already convinced. But I'll take the night to think about it if that's what you want." She bent and removed her hand so she could give him a quick kiss. "Take me home, please. I'm ready."

He stood, towering over her in the darkness. "I didn't say you're beautiful to convince you of anything. I said it because it's true." He brought her hand to his mouth and kissed it. A shiver worked its way down her spine. "You said you're convinced. Can I ask how this happened? A few days ago you could hardly stand the sight of me."

"I didn't know you, did I? I made the mistake of thinking that what I read online was the real you. But then you were so nice to those kids—and, well, everybody who wants to talk to you."

"What did you read online?"

A different kind of heat bloomed across her cheeks. "Well, most of what comes up about you is either about the driving—or the women you date. You're a real heart-breaker, Ross Blackthorne."

"You can't believe everything you read online. But yeah, I've dated a few women. I never promise them anything but a good time though."

"And the champagne baths you routinely give nubile young women?"

He blinked. "Champagne baths... Oh geez, Holly. Those are publicity stunts. Brock hates them, by the way. And it's happened like twice."

"Seriously, you've never *enjoyed* spraying champagne on sexy women who can't wait for a piece of you?"

"Well, I'm not saying I didn't enjoy it. But not nearly as much as I've enjoyed kissing you."

"Ross."

"It's true. Hand to God."

Happiness bloomed in her soul. Whether or not it was

true in the long run, he meant it right now. And that was enough for her in this moment. "Okay. I believe you."

He kissed her hand again. Then he kissed her mouth, but only briefly. No tongues, no heat. "Hey, you hungry?"

Holly laughed. "Another meal together? Do I get to buy this one?"

"Maybe so. You game?"

She thought about it. Spending more time with Ross? Getting to know him even more than she already did? It was a no brainer. Besides, fries and nachos for dinner didn't really cut it.

"Sure, I'm game. But not one mention of business, okay? I want a shot at picking up the bill."

He ushered her back inside so they could lock up before leaving. "I'll try my best."

ROSS WOKE SLOWLY, reluctantly. He'd been having a hot dream about getting naked with Holly and he didn't want it to end. But he knew, as soon as he opened his eyes, that it had most definitely been just a dream.

He was alone in a king-sized bed with white sheets. Light streamed across the bed and he felt around on the nightstand for his phone. Seven a.m.

He groaned. He'd forgotten that the automatic blinds were set to go up at seven on weekdays.

Might as well get up. Ross pushed himself upright, yawning. He reached for the remote and flicked on the television. The TV was already set to his favorite racing channel. Soon they'd be talking about the race this weekend, and then they'd cover practices and qualifying.

He picked up the remote for the blinds and lowered those just a bit. He'd been out late with Holly. After they'd left her old family house, they'd gone to a Waffle House. He'd discovered Waffle Houses when he'd moved to Kentucky. Open all night and serving some of the greasiest food imaginable. Breakfast, burgers, you name it.

He and Holly had taken a booth and ordered breakfast. They'd shared hash browns smothered, covered, chunked, and grilled. Holly explained that meant onions, cheese, ham, and tomatoes. Sounded great to him—and they were.

Over hash browns, eggs, bacon, and coffee, they'd talked about a lot of things. He'd learned that she'd gone to college for a business degree and that she was twenty-seven. Her parents were both dead, her brother was in Connecticut, and of course her sister was in a home in Lexington. She wasn't as tight-lipped about that as she had been the last time they'd discussed it. It made her sad, he knew that, but she'd been more stoic last night. So long as Emily was taken care of, that was the important thing to her.

He didn't tell her that he'd asked Brock to look into her sister's situation. He didn't want to say anything about it in case there was nothing more that could be done.

They'd talked about him too—about his brothers and cousins, about the house in King Harbor and his trips to the distillery as a boy. About his obsession with all things fast, from jet skis to jet boats to racecars. Holly drove the speed limit wherever she went, and he raced to get where he was going. She was a patient person—she had to be in order to be a good distiller since so much of crafting whisky required time, while he was always ready to go balls to the wall with anything he did.

He'd enjoyed last night. He'd even let her pay for the meal since it was under twenty bucks, though he'd left the waitress a big tip because they'd sat there so long and taken up one of her tables. When he'd taken Holly home, they'd sat in her driveway with the engine running and kissed for twenty minutes. He'd been harder than a damned rock when he'd walked her to her door. And he'd called himself a fool for telling her he wasn't going to take advantage of the heat between them just yet.

It was there, and it was hot, and she'd wanted him. So why take it slow? He still didn't know what had made him back off, but something told him not to push this thing too fast. Not to do what he always did and speed through life looking for the next thrill.

Ross wanted to call her just to hear her voice, but it was too damned early. He must have dozed off again because the sound of his phone buzzing jerked him awake a second time. The television was still on and the room was dark because he'd lowered the blinds.

He fished around for his phone, finding it on the bed beneath one of the pillows. It was a text from his cousin, Phillip.

Phillip: *Hey. How's it going in Kentucky?*

Ross: *It's going. How you doing?*

Phillip: *Fine. Just watching some race coverage and thought about you. You okay with not driving this weekend?*

Ross sighed. *Yeah, I'm all right. The distillery is time-consuming.*

Phillip: *Uncle Graham will relent about the racing. He's just grumpy because Aunt Claire hasn't come home yet.*

Ross: *Stubborn old fool needs to go get her.*

Phillip: *He won't. You know that. Blackthorne pride. So, Devlin and Jason. You aren't planning to lose your mind over a woman, right?*

He thought of Holly's silky red hair and blue-gray eyes. The way her breast fit in his hand and how her tongue felt stroking against his. He wanted her, but lose his mind over her? Nah. He was currently obsessed, sure. But he wouldn't stay that way.

Probably wouldn't.

Ross: *Nope.*

Phillip: *Me neither. Glad to hear you're on the same wavelength.*

Ross: *Definitely.*

Phillip: *Oh hell, call coming on the other line. Gotta run. Take care, R.*

Ross: *You too, Philly.*

Phillip: *Don't start, Martin.*

Ross laughed as he tossed the phone down. Phillip hated to be called Philly. Ross had done it when they were kids and he was pissed at his cousin. Phillip had retaliated by calling him Martini & Rossi, which had been funny because they were kids and didn't drink.

Considering the family business was whisky, Phillip had probably picked up the name during one of the many visits they'd had from liquor distributors. He'd eventually shortened it to Martin at Mom's suggestion. She'd probably thought it more appropriate for a kid to use than saying Martini & Rossi all the time.

Ross thought about texting Jason just because, but it was even earlier in LA than it was here. Ross and Jason had always been close, and Ross was happy for his cousin that he'd found a woman who rocked his world. Jason was a first class filmmaker and he'd worked hard for his success. He deserved someone who shared that passion, which Mallory apparently did.

A quick check of the time told him it was after nine now. Ross flipped the covers back and slipped on a pair of athletic shorts before heading for the workout room. He jogged on the treadmill for an hour to get rid of last night's fatty breakfast, then headed into the bathroom where he showered and shaved and got dressed in his favorite faded jeans and a gray henley.

He grabbed a protein bar in the kitchen, then headed out to the eight-car garage—which could actually hold sixteen cars because he had lifts over every bay. He'd only filled twelve of the slots though. He texted Holly before he chose a car.

We still on for today?

It took a few moments before the three dots indicated she was typing something back. Holly had promised to tour the garage today. When he'd left her last night, they'd made a plan that he would pick her up at one. They'd go to lunch, because of course they couldn't miss a meal together, and then they'd head for the garage.

He hadn't exactly told her that he meant his own personal garage and not the racing team's garage, though. Without the team there, it wasn't as interesting as it would be when they returned. So he'd save that trip for another time.

Holly: *Yes. I'll be ready.*

He wanted to ask her about the other part of that conversation last night. The part they'd had on the porch of her old house where she'd said she didn't need to think about sleeping with him. But he wasn't going to do it.

Patience. It was a virtue he was trying to learn.

Ross: *I'm on my way in a few.*

Holly: *Great! Truck or Ferrari?*

Ross: *You don't think those are the only possibilities, do you?*

She sent a laughing emoji. *Fine, surprise me. Just please let it have A/C. It's hot as blazes today.*

Ross: *No problem. I'll leave the steam-driven car in the garage.*

Holly: *Thank God.*

Ross laughed. She accepted that statement like steam-driven cars were a thing. They had been at one time, but they weren't exactly the kind of car you drove on the interstate these days, even if you happened to have one.

He did not. Not fast enough, though he appreciated unique cars.

He selected a C7 ZR-1 Corvette in black with blue accents and blue stitching in the all-black interior. It was a sexy car, and one he enjoyed driving, possibly even more than he did some of the other sports cars he owned.

It was American-made—Kentucky-made, in fact—and front-end heavy because that's where the engine was, but it was still a thing of beauty. And it was less likely to get the kind of attention that a Ferrari or a Lamborghini would get on the road.

It hit him that he shouldn't even be here. He should be in Illinois, speeding around the track in the Blackthorne car—with a Chevrolet engine—but that was Eric's job right now.

He pressed the gas and the Corvette tore down the road. Not like his racecar at all. He missed his car.

And yet he didn't. Because if he was on the track in Joliet, then he wouldn't be on his way to pick up Holly. He wouldn't get to spend the afternoon with her in some random Mom & Pop restaurant that she picked out, and then he wouldn't get to bring her back home and take her through the garage.

He especially wouldn't get to take her inside his house and, God willing, kiss her into quivering submission. If he was lucky, tonight he'd strip Holly naked and explore her body thoroughly. He'd give her pleasure, and he'd take his in return.

No, it wasn't speeding around a track at speeds in excess of two hundred miles per hour. But—shockingly—the thought of making love to Holly was somehow more exhilarating than all the speed in the world.

Chapter 12

"Hols, oh my God, you did not adequately describe the deliciousness of that man!"

It was Mel on the phone, calling to check on her and demand details about last night. Nosy Mel.

"I told you he looked better than his photos."

"I know. Still. Wow. Major hottie alert! Have you seen him up close and personal in his racing silks, or whatever they call them?"

Holly laughed. "Now why would I do that? He's working at the distillery, not racing."

Mel made a noise. "Oh girl. Role-play? You know, make him put that shit on before he seduces you."

"He is not seducing me," she said primly, even while she knew it was a lie. Of course he was. And she'd swung so far in the other direction that she welcomed it. Amazing what a few days in his company could do.

"Puh-leeze. Did you see the way he looked at you last night? Because I did. Holly Brooks, you are the next contestant who gets to saddle up and ride Ross Blackthorne like a bucking bronco!"

"You did not just say that," Holly wheezed. "Oh lord, Mel."

"Oh come on. Of course I did. He wants you. And you want him. Don't deny it."

Holly thought about it. But then she told the truth. "Okay, fine. I do want him. He's sexy and sweet and I like him."

Shockingly.

"He's a billionaire racecar driver and a total player. Don't forget that, girlfriend."

Holly blew out a breath. How could she forget that part? It was front and center in her brain, along with the fact he was a Blackthorne who had control over her future at the distillery if he really wanted it.

But he was also funny and sweet and thoughtful in ways she wouldn't have believed before she'd met him. He was the kind of guy she'd have picked to date if she'd met him somewhere else—and if he wasn't a Blackthorne.

Though apparently being a Blackthorne wasn't quite enough to stop her right now.

"I haven't forgotten. Weren't you just telling me to go for it, by the way? What's with the caution now?"

"Just making sure you know what you're doing."

Did she? Not really. "I'm not going to fall in love with him or anything. I'm just going to see what happens, maybe have some mind-blowing sex, and move on. Nothing wrong with mind-blowing sex, is there?"

Not that she was the type to fall into bed with a guy, but it had been a long time and Ross just seemed to trip all the right switches for her. She *needed* to explore that. Maybe it was risky—hell, downright dangerous—but she had to know.

Mel snorted. "Not in my book. Just so long as you're careful. Do *not* fall for him, Holly."

"I said I wouldn't. Geez, I'm not some sort of desperate virgin who's never been kissed. I haven't had sex in months now. I'm ready. Maybe he's the wrong guy for the big picture, but he's right for right now."

"I just remember how tore up you were over Joshua."

Ah yes, good old Joshua Norton. He'd been good-looking, but he'd known it and he'd acted like he was God's gift. They'd dated for a year before he'd broken up with her because he felt like she gave the distillery more attention than she gave him.

It had taken her a while to realize that what he really wanted was a woman who would take care of him.

"Joshua was a dick. Everybody knew it, including you. I was the one who didn't see it. Are you telling me that a guy who allows little kids to sit in his zillion dollar car is a dick? Because I don't think so. Even if he ends up being bad for me, he's not a jerk."

"Okay, fine. Have fun. And I want *all* the details. Like how big his—"

"Mel!" Holly laughed. "You're awful."

"But you love me."

"I do. How about you? Did you go home with Doug last night? Or did he go home with you? Inquiring minds and all."

Mel sighed. "No, I didn't. He got called into work."

Doug was a firefighter, which meant he worked long hours and had a crazy schedule. Mel had been interested in him forever, but something always happened to prevent them from getting past first base.

"Mel, I don't mean to be, uh, negative or anything—but have you ever considered that maybe there's more going on with Doug than meets the eye? He strings you along and then he always gets called in or has to leave just before things get good."

"Like what? You think he's gay? Or married? Wouldn't somebody know he had a wife and tell me?"

"It might not be either of those things—maybe he's just scared. Or he has erectile dysfunction. Premature ejaculation? I don't know, but you'd think he'd find the time by now."

Mel sighed. "I hate to say you're right, but I think you're right. He said he'd call this weekend. I suppose it's time I asked him what the deal is. If this isn't going anywhere, I need to move on. I've spent enough time waiting for him to make a move."

"Agreed." She heard the rumble of an engine outside and knew it had to be Ross. Nobody in her little neighborhood drove anything that sounded like that. Still, she walked over to the window to look. Something that resembled the Batmobile—or what she thought the Batmobile looked like since she wasn't one hundred percent certain—had pulled into her driveway. A moment later, a tall dark-haired guy in mirrored Oakleys stepped out of the car.

Holly's belly twisted with longing. Oh, my...

"Mel, I have to go. Ross is here."

"Oooh, have fun! And remember, I want details. As many as you'll give me anyway."

"We'll see," Holly said. Then she dropped the phone next to her purse and rubbed her hands down the cute little flippy skirt she'd put on earlier. Panic flared inside. Maybe she should have put on jeans. What was she thinking wearing a skirt? Was she trying too hard?

The doorbell rang. *Too late.*

Holly gulped down nerves and went to the door, her hand closing over the knob. Deep breath in, breathe out. What was wrong with her?

It took her a second, but she tugged the door open slowly, pasting a smile on her face as she did so. Butterflies swirled. Ross was tall, imposing, packed with lean muscle. He wore a gray shirt and faded jeans that hugged him in places few women—straight women—could resist. Add a cowboy hat and boots and he'd look like every woman's cowboy fantasy. As it was, he wore flip flops—manly ones, not cheap ones or plastic ones—and he grinned before his gaze traveled down her body, from the flowery top to the blue swirly skirt and then all the way down her legs to her feet. Thank God she'd had a recent pedicure—rose pink polish, thank you very much.

"Hi," she said.

"Hi. You look terrific."

A blush threatened. "Thank you. So do you." She stepped back. "Would you like to come in?"

He pulled in a breath. Shook his head. "Nope. Because if I do, I won't want to leave anytime soon. I'm going to want to kiss you, then I'll have to slide my hands under that skirt—and, well, if you don't tell me no, then I'm going to undress you and spend the afternoon making you say my name."

Holly's belly tightened. It sounded delicious. And yet... "Okay, I guess I'll get my purse."

"That's a good idea."

She went to grab her purse on shaky legs, then returned and locked up while he waited behind her.

"Where are we going?" he asked when she turned.

"What are you in the mood for?"

His eyes gleamed. "I already told you."

"Food, Ross."

"Ah, food. Surprise me."

"I can do that."

"Believe me, Holly. You already have."

HE WASN'T TALKING about food, either. Holly Brooks was surprising him in more ways than he could currently count. He'd thought her beautiful when he'd seen her striding across the parking lot toward him his first day at the distillery. He'd thought her intriguing when she treated him like a bad rash. His thoughts about her kept expanding and growing and morphing into something that currently amounted to him being consumed by her.

Not a state of affairs he was accustomed to for sure.

Holly Brooks wasn't a model. She wasn't rail thin—she wasn't chubby either—and she wasn't fake in any way that he could tell. She made him wonder how he kept attracting the fake women who put so much stock into their hair and makeup and clothing that he didn't know what mattered to them beyond their appearances.

It wasn't that they weren't pretty. They were. Gorgeously so. He didn't have a thing against makeup and beautiful clothes, or women who looked like they'd stepped out of the pages of a magazine. Hell, he'd dated enough of them and he'd enjoyed it for the most part.

But there was something about Holly and her inability to be nice to him for the sake of being nice to a rich, famous man who could do things for her that pulled at him. If Holly didn't like him, she wouldn't be here. That much he knew. She wasn't capable of faking it, not when her dislike had been so palpable earlier in the week.

Not to mention she hadn't exactly been easy to persuade that he was a nice guy. Up until last night when he'd confronted that ape who'd manhandled her, he hadn't been entirely convinced that she liked him at all, no matter that she'd said she did when he'd fixed her Jeep.

He helped her into the car before going around to his side. She hadn't even tried to stop him opening the door, which was progress. Holly had buckled herself in and she was looking down at her skirt, smoothing it, when he got in. Were her fingers trembling?

"Hey," he said as he pressed the button to start the car.

She jerked her gaze to his. "Hmm?"

Definitely some nerves at work there.

"I'm glad you said yes to this. Today, I mean. I want to show you why I like cars so much."

She smiled. "Well, this one is certainly pretty. I guess I kind of understand. I like making whisky. You like doing things with cars."

"Yeah. I love racing—but I'd like to open my own garage for performance engines. I want to enhance cars for people who can pay—and then I'd like to have another garage where I fix up older cars and match them with people who need something to get back and forth to work or school. When you don't live in a city with good trans- portation, or you live in the country, the difference between making a decent income and being on the streets can come down to having a reliable way to work."

He'd never told anyone that before. He didn't quite know why, but it had seemed like if he said it, people would think he was just saying it to give them a good impression of him. The rich guy with everything giving lip service to doing good works because it looked great on his resume.

But he knew that Holly would understand. She smiled, and his heart skipped.

"Wow. There you go being even more decent. I think that's wonderful, Ross."

"Do you?"

"Of course I do. Who wouldn't?"

"You don't wonder why I don't just buy new cars and give them away?"

She blinked. "Well, I didn't think of that. But I guess

it's because you can fix up a whole lot more older cars for the price of one new one."

He nodded. "That's part of it. The other part is things like insurance and taxes. You give someone a new car, they have to insure it and pay taxes on it. An older car is cheaper."

"Which means you help more people."

"Yeah. Plus if I hire people who need jobs to work in the garage, then I help even more people."

"That's really admirable of you." He thought she sniffled. Then she lifted her head and gave him an exaggerated look. "Geez, Ross, I'm beginning to think maybe you're *too* nice for me."

He snorted. "No way, honey. When it comes to you, I have very specific thoughts that are not nice. Promise, if you stick around, I'll demonstrate them all for you."

"Did you just call me honey?" she asked, eyebrow arched.

"You know I did."

She laughed. "I'll allow it. This time. So when are you opening this garage where you help people?"

"I don't know yet."

"What's stopping you from doing it now? You have the money. You know people."

He glanced at her. She was waiting for the answer, but he didn't really have one. It was something he wanted to do, but he kept putting off the garage—both sides of it—because he was so busy racing. But maybe it was time. Maybe he needed to use this break from the racing team to do what he'd been telling himself he would do for years now.

"I guess I thought I was too busy to give it the attention it needed. I keep saying every year that I'll get it done in the off-season. But I never do. It's time I made it a priority."

Holly's smile was huge. "That's how you do things, Ross. A step at a time. Just like making whisky."

———

"YOUR RACING GARAGE IS HERE?" Holly asked, puzzled.

They'd gone out for Italian food and now they were headed toward his garage. Except the area of Louisville he was driving through was very exclusive. It featured large homes with wrought iron fences and gates that were designed to shut people out. She couldn't imagine a garage around here, and yet Ross was driving down the street like they'd pull up to one at any moment.

"Well, not quite," he said as he pressed a button on the visor. A pair of iron gates rolled open as he turned into a driveway that went up a gentle hill. At the top sat a huge mansion that looked a bit like a French chateau. It was surrounded by mature trees and gorgeous landscaping.

"Here? You're working on a stock car here?"

He laughed. "No, not here."

They passed beneath an archway and into a motor court with a huge garage that featured eight doors. *Eight doors*. She turned to gape at him.

"Home sweet home," he said.

"Ross. Holy hell, this is…"

"Ostentatious?"

"Well, maybe? But no, I was going to say it's huge… Maybe even overwhelming."

One of the garage doors cranked up and Ross drove inside. The garage itself was light because there were transom windows set high along one wall. It was also gleaming. The floors were white, the walls were white, and it was filled with cars, some stacked on lifts above others. She saw the Ferrari. The truck. And others that she didn't even know what they were. A BMW over there. A Porsche?

Ross Blackthorne wasn't just rich. He was ridiculously, fabulously wealthy.

Holly swallowed. She didn't know how to process this. Of course she knew he was rich. But seeing it like this—well, it was even more shocking than a two million dollar car.

Except how it was more shocking she wasn't sure—it just was. A car was a small thing. But a house like this one. All these cars in one place.

Yeah, wow. Just wow.

And he'd brought her here. Like they were on a date. Little Holly Brooks who put on overalls and a bandanna and got down into the mash when she had to. Distilling whisky could be a messy business sometimes, and she did it all. She wasn't the kind of woman who fit in a place like this.

"The racing team is in Illinois this weekend. There's nothing to see at the garage there, so I brought you here. It's not the same thing, but it's mine and these are my cars."

"I didn't know it was possible for one person to have so many cars."

He shut off the Corvette and opened his door. "I told you they've been my obsession since I was a kid. Come on, let me show you around."

Holly stepped onto the spotless floor. You could eat off it if you wanted. Ross came over and took her hand. They walked through the gleaming garage while he opened car doors for her and told her about each one. A Bugatti Veyron, a Porsche 911 GT3, an Audi R-8, a Mercedes

AMG something or other, a McLaren convertible in the prettiest deep maroon she'd ever seen, and several others that ran together in her head. He knew everything there was to know—the zero to sixty times, the production numbers, the horsepower, the special thing about each car that made him want to own it.

He had older cars, too. An Italian import called a De Tomaso Pantera was shiny red and gleaming. The interior was black, and all the original knobs were there. The engine was in the back of the car—which he called mid-engine—and it was made by Ford.

"By Ford? I thought you said this is an Italian car."

"It is. But Ford made the engines. Ford imported the car and sold it here. There were about seven-thousand of them made."

"Do you drive all these cars?"

He nodded. "Yep. They're each fun in their own way. It's a different experience depending on which car you drive. I like the variety."

Like he liked a variety of women?

Holly dropped her gaze and nibbled the inside of her lip. She was out of her depth with this man. Hopelessly out of her depth. Maybe this was a mistake. Maybe she needed to ask him to take her home and forget all about spending more time with him.

He tipped her chin up. That single touch, the way her body responded, told her she wasn't going to leave. She didn't want to.

"I'm sorry. It's too much for one visit, right?" he asked.

"No, it's really not, honest. But it's so much information. I don't know how you keep it all sorted in your head."

He gave her a grin, one eyebrow arching. "Kinda like you and the distillery. I don't know how you keep all that sorted, or how you know just what to do or order or who to talk to. It's a much bigger job than remembering facts about cars."

"It's important to you just like the whisky is important to me. I think I understand why you wanted me to see your cars now."

"Why?"

"To prove that when we love a thing, it comes easy to us. Running the distillery comes easy to me. It's what I was born to do."

"In a way, I was born to do it too. But it's not natural for me. I don't love it."

"Okay, so we have to have passion for it. You're passionate about cars. I'm passionate about whisky."

He tugged her into his arms. Her hands went up to press against his chest. Her stomach clenched and her pulse careened. "I'm passionate about you, Holly Brooks. I want—desperately—to take you to bed. You're not like any woman I've ever met."

Her heart sped in her chest like one of his cars careening around a track. It raced so fast she thought she was going to be dizzy with it.

But this was it. The moment of truth. Did she say yes? Or did she push back and ask for more time? Because if she said no, he would respect that.

She thought of Mel. She could hear her friend's voice in her head telling her to go for it. And to be careful, of course. *Don't fall for him.*

No, she wasn't going to fall for him. And though another part of her kept insisting it was a bad idea to get involved with a Blackthorne, she wasn't listening.

This wasn't involved. It was sex. She could have sex.

She pulled in a breath. "Yes," she said. "I want that too."

He lowered his head and kissed her. It wasn't a

desperate kiss, though she wanted it to be. It was soft, sweet. Restrained. She tried to get closer, kiss harder. If she was going to do this, she wanted to do it at full tilt—before her nerves got the best of her.

But he eased her away from him and brushed her hair back from her shoulders. "I'm going to do this right," he said. "Not rip your clothes off and take you in a garage."

Holly curled her fingers into his shirt. "I'm not a virgin, Ross. You don't have to make this into some sort of long drawn-out seduction like we're in *Downton Abbey*."

His eyes widened. Then he laughed. "I wasn't trying to. I just want you to be comfortable. You seemed nervous earlier."

"Of course I'm nervous. I've never had sex with you before. And I want to, which still scares me. But not enough to make me tell you to take me home. I want this. I want *you*."

He searched her gaze. "You really do, don't you? You want *me*."

"I said that didn't I?"

She didn't know what he was thinking, or what he would say—but then he moved, sweeping her legs from beneath her, lifting her. Holly squeaked as she wrapped her arms around his neck. He started moving, striding through the garage with purpose. His expression was fierce as he stopped and punched in a code—and a door swung open, leading into the darkened interior of a hallway.

Holly barely got a glimpse of the rooms as he strode through them. They were stark though. Modern. There was nothing personal in any of the main rooms they passed through. She glimpsed a turquoise pool outside the living room, a raised area she assumed was a hot tub, and a waterfall.

Ross didn't stop for any of it. He carried her through a

door and into the biggest bedroom she'd ever seen in her life. A king-sized bed sat against the far wall, and there was at least an acre of floor between it and the door. The windows opened onto a landscaped view that included the pool.

Ross took her over to the bed and laid her down on it, kneeling over her as he did so. He reached for something on the bedside table, and the room started to grow darker as shades dropped slowly down over the bright windows.

Then he tossed the remote aside and reached for the hem of his shirt. Holly's mouth went dry as the ridges of his abdomen appeared. His shirt fell over the side of the bed—and then he stretched out, holding himself above her, barely pressing any weight into her body at all.

"You still sure?" he asked softly.

Holly's gaze flicked over his face, searching for... what? She did not know. His eyes were smoky brown, serious, and she knew that if she said no, even now, he'd stop. In spite of their position, in spite of the insistent press of his groin against hers, Ross would lever himself up and put his shirt on again if she asked.

She wasn't going to ask.

"Yes," she said. "I'm sure."

Chapter 13

Ross let out the breath he'd been holding. Because he'd known it was entirely possible Holly would change her mind—if her very logical brain started reminding her about all those internet articles she'd read and photos she'd seen. If she started thinking about the fact he was a Blackthorne.

But she hadn't. She'd said yes. He practically groaned with relief.

Then he dropped his mouth to hers, dying to taste her, dying to give her everything he could. Her mouth opened, warm and wet and welcoming. Her arms went around his neck—and then she opened her legs and wrapped them around him too.

Oh God, heaven.

Her crotch hit him right where he most wanted pressure and he groaned. His dick was aching to be free. To slide into her and take them both to nirvana.

Patience.

Holly deserved his best.

He cupped her breast. She didn't have a bountiful

chest, but in his mind she had a perfect one. Just enough to fit in his hand. Beautiful, firm, perfect.

He skimmed his hand down her side. Her skirt was bunched at her hips because it had fallen when she'd put her legs around him. He took full advantage, stroking her bare thigh, the edge of her panties. Not a thong. And not silky. A nice, simple cotton panty that was probably white.

So very Holly. No nonsense. Serious. With a plan and a job to do.

He had a plan too.

Long, slow, wet, deep kisses. He focused on those until he was about to burst. Then he levered upright and helped her to her feet beside the bed. She swayed a little and he caught her close, feeling protective and fierce all at once.

"Need to get this off," he said, tugging her shirt upward. She cooperated, putting her hands above her head. He shook out her shirt and laid it on a chair so it wouldn't wrinkle. She watched him with a wry expression.

"What?" he asked.

"Thoughtful," she said. She reached out and put a palm on his stomach. His skin sizzled as her small hands ran over the ridges of his abdomen. "So not fair."

"What?" he asked stupidly.

"You. This body."

"You don't like it?"

"Are you kidding me? Of course I like it. But some of the things you eat, Ross—you should have to fight a little harder to look like this."

He put his fingers in the waistband of her skirt, looking for a zipper or a button. Found a hidden zipper at the side, along with a hook. "I work out," he said, dropping his mouth to her neck as she tilted her head back. "Hard."

She shuddered. Her palms skimmed up his chest, over

his pecs. She pinched a nipple softly, and sensation streaked to his groin.

"So hard," she whispered.

"*Very* hard," he growled, sliding the zipper down after he'd released the hook. The skirt fell to the floor. And as much as he didn't want to stop what he was doing, he picked that up as she stepped out of it and placed it with her shirt.

When he turned back to her, his breath arrested. Holly Brooks was a goddess. How had he ever—*ever*—thought that the overly polished kind of women he often met on the circuit were beautiful? Because they weren't. At least not like Holly—in her simple white cotton panties and white lace bra.

She looked at him shyly. Her lashes dropped and he could see her pulse thrumming in her throat.

Go to her.

He moved, swept her against him before she could begin to think that she was somehow lacking. Because she would. He knew that about her.

"I have never seen anything so damned sexy," he said, his voice hoarse and choked and filled with some kind of emotion that shocked him.

"You don't have to say—" she began.

He hushed her with a kiss. After a moment, the heat between them flared so hot that Holly started to fumble for the buttons on his fly. She got them undone and then he reached down and shoved his jeans off, stepping out of them as he lifted her onto the bed.

"I want inside you so bad," he told her.

"I want that too."

"I have condoms."

"So do I."

He pushed onto an elbow and looked down at her. At

her pale skin and pretty red hair. So lovely. He trailed his finger down her chest, then pushed it beneath one of the cups on her bra.

"I should have known." Carefully, he exposed her nipple. "Beautiful," he said as he lowered his head and skimmed his tongue around the tight little bud.

"Oh," she gasped. "Please don't stop."

"Don't intend to. Not until you're limp and can't take anymore."

———

HOLLY THOUGHT her heart would burst from her chest at any second. Ross sucked her nipple into his mouth and pleasure spiked hard inside her. There was an electric current flowing between them, engulfing her wholly, snapping between her nipple and her sex, making her entire body quiver like a frightened virgin's.

She was anything but frightened. She was desperate, needy, aching with pent up sexual frustration.

Ross reached beneath her and unsnapped her bra. She'd worn the prettiest matching set she had, but they were still white and plain. She hadn't thought about that until she'd been getting dressed this morning. It'd been too late to run to the mall and hit up the Victoria's Secret for something sexier, so here she was.

She'd kind of expected he'd take her to lunch and the garage and then maybe they'd return to her house where she could contrive to get undressed when he wasn't looking.

Like that would have happened. It was obvious to her now that there was no excusing oneself to strip when things were as hot as they currently were.

Besides, Ross didn't seem deterred by her underwear.

When he'd turned to look at her after laying out her skirt —really, she couldn't get over the fact he'd considered how her clothing might wrinkle on the floor—the look on his face had caused something hot and joyful to flare deep inside.

But then she'd started to overthink it, wondering if she was wrong, if he was more shocked than aroused. Until he'd told her he'd never seen anything so sexy. Whether or not he meant it, Ross Blackthorne was smooth and knew just what to say at the right moment.

She chose to believe he meant it. The kind of man who put her clothing on a chair so it didn't wrinkle wasn't the kind of guy to only be thinking about himself.

His hands—not quite as soft as she'd thought they might be, thanks to working with car engines—flowed over her skin like rainwater, seeking all her hollows. She rose to him, pressed her body to his, chasing the pleasure he left in his wake.

When he hooked his thumbs into her panties and tugged, she lifted her hips for him, her body on edge. She was so ready for this.

He nearly choked and she opened her eyes to find him looking at her panties.

"They're lacy in the back. See-through."

"Yes," she said with a grin.

"Well, hell. I want to see that. Later," he added as he dropped them over the side of the bed. His gaze skimmed her body. "So damned gorgeous."

He dropped a kiss to her stomach, traced his tongue around her belly button, and then he was moving south again. When he pushed her legs open and settled between them, Holly thought she might die.

Smoky brown eyes met hers over the delta of her body. "Strap in for the ride. It's gonna get intense."

He wasn't lying. From the moment he touched his tongue to her sex, stars sparked and flared behind her eyelids. It didn't take long for Holly to fly apart, her body melting beneath his.

He took her to the edge again, and she flew high and far before coming back to earth. Then he rolled his way up her body in a wave of kisses and caresses. She reached for him, realized he hadn't shed his underwear yet.

She lifted her head off the pillow to look—and yes, praise heaven, boxer briefs. The white material clung to his hips, his firm thighs. The prominent bulge in the center was large and defined. Holly slipped her hands into his briefs, wrapped a hand around him.

Ross stilled. Groaned as she stroked him.

"These need to go," she said.

"Hell yes," he muttered. But he still didn't move. Holly did. She pushed the briefs off, tried to push Ross over onto his back so she could repay the favor.

But he stopped her.

"Not this time, baby," he said, reaching for the drawer in the bedside table. He dragged out a strip of condoms and tore one off before dropping them on the bed.

"Let me," she said, taking the package from him. She tore it open and sheathed him while he held himself still above her.

He sank into her slowly, carefully, and she held her breath as she gazed up at him, her heart throbbing and her belly swirling with heat. Their eyes never left each other's face.

"You feel so good," he said when he'd slid all the way inside her. "You okay?"

She touched his cheek. She couldn't seem to help it. Ross turned his face into her hand. Kissed her palm. "Yes," she said. "I'm fine."

"I'm not. If I don't move, I'm gonna explode."

"Yes. Please, *please* move."

She rose up to him and he took her mouth in a kiss that removed all restraint between them. He moved, slow at first, then plunging into her again and again, their bodies rising and falling together as the flames of their pleasure licked at them.

The pressure intensified, the fire burning higher, faster, brighter—nothing had ever felt this good. No man had ever made her feel like this. Hot, crazy, desperate.

Alive.

Holly got there first, flying over the edge for the third time since he'd laid her on the big bed. She wrapped her arms around him, threaded her fingers in his hair, and kissed him so hard their teeth clashed. He moaned and thrust harder, deeper.

She knew when he came. His body stiffened and he groaned into her mouth, feeding her back the moans she'd given him. Finally, she tore her mouth from his, gulping in air and wondering if she'd ever be able to move again.

Waiting for the regret that never came.

They lay there, entangled in each other, breathing heavily into the silence. Ross pressed his mouth to her neck, her shoulder, then he dipped down to lick a nipple before he disentangled himself from her and went to dispose of the condom.

She watched him return, admiring the long lines of his body. The tight, lean muscle that made him worthy of a sculpture. He was still half hard, and she admired that too. She'd be a little sore, probably—but oh, it was so worth it.

Ross started at the foot of the bed and panther-crawled his way up her body, grinning the entire time. Holly grinned back.

"That was *incredible*, sugar. You're incredible."

"Sugar?" she said with an arched brow. But she wasn't really mad. It was impossible to be mad after the way he'd made her feel.

He kissed the tip of her nose. Like she was cute or something. "Yeah, you taste like sugar. Sugar and spice and everything nice."

She laughed as he rolled them to the side so they faced each other, propping himself on an elbow over her. "I'll allow it this time," she said primly. "Sweet cheeks."

"Sweet cheeks? What the hell?"

"Oh yes, I watched your ass as you walked away. Sweet. Cheeks."

"Damn, girl. Way to objectify a dude."

"If only I had a bottle of champagne to spray…"

He snorted. "Fine, you win." His gaze dropped to her breasts. She tried not to feel self-conscious, but she kinda did. She'd seen what he dated before. Not that they were dating.

"What do I win?"

His gaze lifted to hers. "Me," he said.

Then he pulled her to him. She forgot about feeling self-conscious for the next hour.

Chapter 14

Ross watched Holly circle through his living room, touching furniture and gazing out the windows at the pool. He wished he'd talked her into packing a bag so she could stay the whole weekend. Now that he'd made love to her, he was more addicted than before.

Holly was real in a way he wasn't accustomed to. She wasn't a model or an actress or any of the women he usually encountered at races, race events, and Blackthorne charity events. Holly was simply herself, and she had strong opinions and no intention of liking the things he liked just to please him.

Which, ironically enough, pleased him.

She looked up and caught him staring. He was standing by the island, sending texts to Martin and Eric. Except he'd forgotten to press send and he was just staring.

A slow smile wreathed her face. "What?"

"You. You're gorgeous and you're in my house. And I've had sex with you twice now, which really makes me happy."

She ducked her head, tucking her hair behind her ear,

and he knew she was blushing. "Such a flatterer," she said softly. Teasingly.

But he wasn't flattering her. He was happy. Happier than he'd expected to be with his team in Joliet and him here. He still had time to make the points for the play-offs, or what used to be called the chase, but he wasn't really thinking about it. He was thinking about her. About what it felt like to be buried inside her, moving as one.

Heaven.

He didn't want that to end.

"Hey, what do you think about staying the night? We can order in. Maybe swim a little. If you stay until Sunday, we can watch the race together."

She shook her head. "I can't stay. I don't have any clothes."

"You won't need clothes. I'll loan you a robe if you don't want to walk around naked. Though I approve of naked."

"Very funny. I mean I don't want to put on the same underwear tomorrow."

"I have a washer and dryer. We can fix this."

"What do I swim in?"

"Nothing?"

She folded her arms. "No, not nothing."

"I'll have somebody pick up a suit from the mall. It can be here in an hour tops."

Her jaw dropped. "You can do that?"

He shrugged. "Well, yeah. So what do you say?"

She nibbled her lip. "How about we go to Walmart and I'll buy a suit?"

He didn't know why she was so reluctant to accept things from him. "Does that mean you'll stay?"

"I shouldn't."

"Why not? The distillery is closed until Monday— except for the tours, but you aren't needed for those."

He pressed send and tossed his phone on the counter, oblivious to any return texts, and walked over to put his hands on her hips, pull her gently to him. She tilted her head back, her palms resting on his chest. "Stay with me, Holly. Just for tonight. I can take you home tomorrow if you want to go."

"And if I say no?" she whispered.

She wasn't going to say no. He could feel it. "I'll take you home tonight."

"I feel out of place here," she said, and his heart clenched.

"Why?"

She rolled her gaze around the cavernous room. "This house. It's so much bigger than I expected."

He frowned. "The house? Is that all?"

She met his eyes. "I, uh, I'm not the kind of woman who fits in a house like this. I feel like Beyoncé should glide down those giant stairs in the front entrance with a beam of light shining on her while a fan blows her hair."

He squeezed her. "Holly. You fit. It's just a house. I know it's huge—and I've decided I hate the decor, by the way. But I bought it because of the garage. I need a big garage for my cars."

She blinked. "Seriously? You bought a mansion for the garage?"

"Told you I was a gear head." He shot her a cheeky smile.

"That's crazy."

"I know." He pushed her hair off her shoulders, loving the way the silky strands felt in his fingers. "So will you stay? I promise not to make you walk down the stairs like Beyoncé. Unless you want to, of course…"

She slapped him playfully. "I do *not* want to."

He kissed her. "Stay, Holly," he said between kisses. "Don't make me sleep in that big bed alone."

She moaned as he swiped his tongue in her mouth. "Ross, you don't play fair."

"Nope. Fair isn't how you win."

"Okay, I'll stay—but only if you take me to Walmart so I can buy some things."

"Fine. Walmart. We'll take the Lambo."

She laughed as she clutched his shoulders and he tilted her back. "No, no fancy cars. Don't you have a plain old Toyota or something?"

"I've got a Toyota."

"Then we can take that."

"Okay, baby. Whatever you say."

ROSS'S TOYOTA WAS A SEQUOIA–NORMAL enough —but he'd supercharged it. Which meant it was fast. Very fast. They sped through town to the Walmart where Holly picked up a swimsuit, new underwear, and a couple of tank tops and some shorts. She also grabbed some toiletries and mascara. The whole thing cost less than fifty bucks. Ross tried to pay but she wouldn't let him.

They returned to his house and she marveled again at the size of it. It was beautiful, but stark inside. The furniture had clean lines and sleek finishes, but nothing said sit down and put your feet up. It felt like a museum, not a place anyone lived.

"You don't like the furniture, do you?" he asked when they were sitting at the giant kitchen island eating the pizza he'd ordered.

"I, um." She swallowed a bite of pizza. "It's very clean."

He laughed. "That's one way of putting it. So what would you do if it was your house?"

She blinked. "Well, I can't imagine having a house this big, but I think I'd fill it with comfortable furniture and books. You have all those built-in bookshelves, but nothing on them except for statuary and decorative plates."

"I hired a designer and told her to do what she wanted."

He didn't seem too happy about it either.

"Well there's your issue. But what do you like, Ross? Where are your trophies and car stuff? Maybe some of those would look good in here."

"They're in the man cave. That's my favorite room. Guess I still need to give you the tour." He waggled his eyebrows. "I was more interested in getting you naked, though."

Which she hadn't minded in the least.

"Well, I'm glad you have them displayed somewhere. But you could still warm this room up with books and stuff."

"And the rest of the house?"

Holly gave him a wry look. "Ross, I'm a whisky maker, not an interior designer. Hire a different one—one who believes a house is meant to be lived in rather than magazine ready."

He looked around. "I guess I thought I might sell it at some point anyway so why bother."

Her heart flipped. She'd always known he wasn't staying, but she didn't like to hear it so soon after they'd been together for the first time. "Where would you go if you sold this house?"

"I dunno. I'd always thought North Carolina. I

intended to take the team there, once we'd grown a bit more and I could replace Martin Temple. Not that I've found a suitable replacement for him—and not that I'm racing at the moment."

She tried to smile. "Sounds like a plan. When your dad relents."

His gaze seemed to sharpen. "Or maybe I could move to Lexington. Be closer to the distillery."

"That's an option," she said evenly. "Assuming you're going to be there a while."

"I might be." He took a drink of the beer he'd opened. "Would that bother you? If I were there, I mean."

Nerves fluttered to life in her belly. "Why would it bother me? You're a Blackthorne. It's always been your destiny if you wanted it."

He seemed to accept that. He twisted the bottle of beer in his hands. "What about you? Would you ever consider moving away from Kentucky?"

Holly's throat tightened. "No. I'm a bourbon maker. This is where I belong. My sister is here. Uncle Evan and Aunt Brenda. All my friends. I wouldn't fit in anywhere else."

"I think you'd fit in wherever you went, Holly. You're competent and determined. There's not a company alive that wouldn't hire you if they needed something done."

She glowed a little at his praise. "You mean a distillery. That's all I know how to do."

"You'd be surprised how those skills translate—especially to a company that's willing to train you to do something else."

She tilted her head. "Are you trying to get me to change careers or what?"

"Not at all. Just pointing out that you could. If you wanted to."

"I don't want to."

He nodded. "I got that." The silence stretched for a long moment. "Your brother changed careers. How did that happen?"

Holly swallowed. "Ricky never wanted to work at the distillery. Or at least that's what I believe. He got a dual degree in business and chemistry, then came home and started working. My dad and uncle always thought he'd be the one to take over. Because he was a man, of course. Girls don't run distilleries."

Ross was frowning. "You do."

It pleased her he'd realized that since Uncle Evan was technically in charge. "I do now. But they were old school, different era, all that crap. They believed that a man—a Brooks man—would be the logical heir. Didn't matter that Ricky only half cared about distilling whisky. He's a great bullshitter and they fell for it."

"That must have bothered you a lot."

"You have no idea. It's bad enough when people think you can't do something as well as a man because you're a woman. It's worse when it's your own family."

"Your uncle doesn't seem to think that way now. He told me you were the best he had."

Her chin notched up with pride. "Because I am. And because he had a come-to-Jesus moment when the fire destroyed everything."

"How did the fire happen?"

She was still bitter and she knew it. "How do they usually happen? Lightning hit one of the barrelhouses. Once it went up, the other two followed. They were too close together. I'd argued for plowing some of our profits into building new barrelhouses, farther apart, but Ricky said it wasn't time. That we had enough separation and it'd be fine until we got bigger. Dad and Uncle Evan listened to him instead of me. It wasn't fine."

"He left the business after you sold to my dad."

"Yes. I mean I love my brother, but getting out of the whisky business was the best thing for him. It takes patience—and he doesn't have any. So he took a job in Connecticut with a drug company. I don't know what he's doing there, but he's happier. Met his wife last year. They have a baby on the way."

"And your sister? She's the youngest. Did she care about whisky the way you do?"

Holly smiled sadly. "She did. We were going to buy Ricky out when we inherited someday and run the distillery together."

"And now she can't. Do you think she could ever move out of the group home?"

"Anything is possible if the right therapy or procedure or drug were to come along. But it hasn't. She's too dependent on help, and the staff there is really good. She also has some behavioral issues stemming from the injury. She's safer there."

Ross reached out and put his hand over hers. Her skin immediately grew hot where he touched her. "You're a strong woman, Holly Brooks. You've had a lot of problems to shoulder—and now you've got me to deal with, too."

She leaned forward and kissed him, needing the contact. Needing to put away her sadness and feel happy in the moment. "Yeah, but now I know how to deal with you."

When she would have pulled away, he tugged her back for a longer, hotter kiss. As if he knew what she needed.

"You certainly do."

Those were the last words they spoke for some time.

SHE DEFINITELY KNEW how to deal with him. Ross lay in bed, body sated, mind whirling. Holly slept beside him, curled on her side, her hair spilling over the pillows like a river of red flame against his white sheets.

He liked seeing her there. Liked the way she made his house seem less empty and more lively. After pizza, they'd climbed in the hot tub and he'd queued up a movie on the giant television screen under the portico.

Talladega Nights, of course. Holly had laughed through all of Ricky Bobby's antics. Between laughing and watching the movie, they'd talked about nearly everything.

Politics, religion—the big no-no topics, but they mostly agreed on those subjects—books, whisky, food, cars, hobbies, favorite season, favorite color, favorite holiday, etcetera.

Ross loved the way the lights in the hot tub made her glow—her skin was luminescent, her hair vibrant. He loved the way she laughed when Ricky Bobby did something funny, the way she seemed to throw everything she was into everything she did.

He'd thought her reserved and standoffish when he'd met her. He'd thought her cold and mean.

It was so far from the truth as to be laughable. Holly Brooks was sweet, vibrant, and lovely. There were sweet, vibrant, lovely women in his circles too. Most of them were married. Then there were other women who, no matter how beautiful, always seemed to be trying to project an image of who they wanted to be—or who he might want them to be—rather than being themselves.

He loved that Holly was herself.

He turned over and put a hand on her hip. She stirred and sighed but didn't wake.

He loved being inside her body. The way she made him feel—it was something special, he knew that. Something big. He couldn't define it, not yet, but he knew it wasn't a feeling he wanted to give up anytime soon. He needed Holly in his life and in his bed, for however long they made each other feel good.

He pressed a kiss to her naked shoulder.

He hadn't wanted to work at the distillery. He still didn't feel like it was his calling in life. But he had to admit, if he hadn't flamed out on the track and roused his dad's ire, he'd have never known Holly.

Somehow, that would have been even worse than not racing.

Chapter 15

Holly was sitting at her desk on Monday morning when her phone rang. She picked it up, saw the name, and shook her head.

"Hello, Mel," she said.

"Girlfriend, you'd better spill. You spent all weekend with that man! Don't tell me you didn't do a little mattress mambo."

Holly laughed. God, Mel cracked her up. Or maybe it was just easy to laugh right now. She was happy. She felt bubbly and light inside, like maybe she'd fly away if she didn't concentrate on staying on the ground. Ross did that to her. Who would have dreamed it a week ago?

"I'm not telling you anything."

"Holly Margaret Brooks, you are a terrible friend. Fine, I'll tell you about mine. Doug called and we talked. I asked him what was wrong and if he just didn't like me."

"And?"

"I'm considering not telling you. You'd deserve it if I didn't."

Holly rolled her eyes. "Okay, fine. Yes, we did it.

Several times. He's magnificent and I'm very satisfied. Happy?"

"Not quite, but that'll do if it's all you're telling me."

"Come over some night this week and let's have some wine. I'll tell more when I'm liquored up, I'm sure."

"Now you're talking! Anyway, Doug. He has a stutter and he didn't want me to know. When he's at the bar, he has a beer and it relaxes him enough that it's not noticeable at all. When he called me, he'd had two. But he thought if we left the bar together, that I'd be turned off once we were somewhere quieter and I could hear the stutter."

Holly's heart ached for him. "Aw, poor guy. Not that he stutters, just that he thought you'd care. You don't care, right?"

Mel seemed a little shocked. "Of course not!"

"Sorry, I didn't mean to suggest you would. I know you don't."

"Of course I don't. But, girl, you should have had all the ornery worked out of you by Mr. Sexy Racy Pants."

Holly snorted. "Well, I definitely did. I'm just a bit distracted is all. I apologize. So are you seeing Doug now? Did you get together?"

"Not yet. He really did have to work a shift this weekend. But we're going out tomorrow night. Dinner at a restaurant. Quieter than a bar."

"That's great."

"Sooo," Mel said, dragging it out a little bit. "Are you seeing Ross now? Or was it a weekend of bliss and we're moving on now?"

Holly felt her skin heating. She was glad Ross had his own office unlike the first couple of days when he'd been in here with her. If she had to look at him right this second, she'd burst into flame. "He was still interested this morning when he kissed me in the barrel house. So I'm thinking maybe we're seeing each other. For now anyway."

"I knew it. He'd be a fool not to want you."

"Well, let's not start booking venues and ordering dresses, okay? We're having sex. It's not permanent."

It hurt to say that. She didn't know why it hurt, but it did. And yet she had to remind herself of it. Often. Because Ross was still trying to get back to racing. And once he did—because she had no doubt, now that she'd seen his house and all his trophies, that he *would* go back— whatever was going on between them would be over.

They'd watched the race on Sunday, and he'd explained about series and points and playoffs, which she'd thought was called the chase for some reason, until she couldn't keep it all straight. But the basic thing she remembered was the travel. More than thirty races from February to November. Just about every weekend. There was no way to continue a relationship, even just a sexual one, if he was gone all the time.

If Ross went back to racing, they were done. For a woman who'd wanted him gone from the distillery just a few days ago, that thought certainly made her stomach tighten.

"Okay, fine, not permanent. But I called it. He was interested in you. I knew he had to be."

Holly's mouth twisted in a wry grin. "Yes, you were right. Do you want a prize?"

"Sure. How about a bottle of Blackthorne Brooks Creek Select? Or even just good old Blackthorne Select. Whatever."

"I'll see what I can do. I might know some people."

They talked a few more minutes and then Holly had to go for a meeting with Uncle Evan and the team. Ross was in the meeting too. He was kicked back in a chair at one end of the table, fingers lazily moving back and forth against his lower lip, his eyes intent on her.

"Holly," Uncle Evan said at one point in the meeting. "Are you feeling okay?"

"What? Of course I am. Why wouldn't I be?"

"You're a little red."

"It's hot in here," she blurted.

"I agree," Ross chimed in. "Definitely hot."

"I'll check the thermostat," one of the guys said as he got up.

Truthfully, it was colder than the Arctic, but the way Ross stared at her made her warm. More than warm. Blazing hot. All she could do was imagine the way he'd looked naked—and the way he'd taken her to heaven with his mouth and body.

So many times this weekend. *So many times.*

She wanted a repeat. As soon as possible.

By the looks of him, he did too.

When five o'clock rolled around, the distillery began to empty out. Holly packed up her stuff and walked out of the office. Ross was coming out of his. He looked so fine in his Blackthorne polo and jeans, and she took a moment to appreciate just how lucky she was that she knew that body intimately.

He gave her a heated look. "Have a good day at the office, Holly?"

Goofball. He'd been with her for a lot of it. "I sure did. How about you?"

"It was fine. Not as good as tonight's going to be, though."

"Really? Do you have plans?"

They were walking down the hallway, passing open office doors. Then they hit the stairs and headed down to the ground level.

"Yep. Going to take my lady to dinner and then I'm going to take her back to her place for dessert. Lots of dessert. Hot, sticky, sweet dessert."

She was sweating. Even her hair was hot. Geez. "Oh yeah? Sounds nice. I'm sure she'll be thrilled."

They walked out into the parking lot. Since it was quitting time, the lot was filled with people talking and getting into their cars.

Ross went over to the truck he'd driven today and she went to her Jeep. They were parked beside each other, their driver doors side by side because he'd backed in.

"I want to kiss you," he said as he stood with his hand on the door.

"I want it too." They couldn't though because she'd insisted she didn't want everyone knowing she was sleeping with the Blackthorne in their midst. Ross had agreed, but she didn't think he liked being a secret.

Still, it'd only been one weekend. Anything could happen.

"Then we'd better get out of here."

"You know what, Ross?" she said as she opened her door. "Why don't you go straight to your lady's house and give her that dessert before dinner?"

He arched an eyebrow. "You think she'd like that?"

"Oh yeah. She'd be crazy not to."

A COUPLE OF DAYS LATER, Ross trailed after Holly as they walked through the facility on their way to bottling. He liked following her so he could watch her ass. That ass he'd had his hands on every night this week. Those legs that had wrapped around him while he lost all his control and gave her everything he had.

162

He'd been at the distillery for almost two weeks now. And it wasn't all that bad. Or maybe it was Holly who made it not bad. He didn't know, but he'd actually been a little fascinated by the process lately. It was like he hadn't fully appreciated it until he'd been forced to spend a few days working with every part of the process of distilling whisky.

Yes, it required patience, but there was a definite art to it. And satisfaction when you tasted something you'd made. Something very fine.

He could see it in Holly's face whenever they tasted the whisky to see if it was ready yet. She had a real pride in what she did. He drove cars, but pride wasn't a part of it. He did it because he loved speed. He loved winning, too.

But pride didn't figure into it for him. He won trophies and points and money, but that wasn't the same as creating something that gave people a lot of pleasure.

Oh, sure, he could argue that watching him race gave people pleasure. But it wasn't the same thing. He didn't create a thing people loved, and nobody got to participate in his success or failures except for him and his team. That wasn't the same as someone cracking open a bottle of their favorite Blackthorne whisky and sharing with friends because they'd gotten promoted or had a baby or gotten engaged or started a business.

He'd heard from Brock earlier today. The information wasn't what he'd hoped. Emily Brooks treated for a brain injury and she was in a home for people who couldn't live on their own. That was all the information he could get, which was less than Holly had told him. Emily'd had to relearn how to feed herself and tie her shoes and everything else that people like him took for granted.

Her family visited her once a week. Evan, his wife, and Holly alternated who went because Emily could only see one person at a time. More wasn't good for her because their presence agitated her. Emily had said she had behavioral issues, but she hadn't elaborated.

Ross had nearly choked up. His family irritated the shit out of him sometimes, but they had his back all the time and that was worth more than every drop of Blackthorne Gold they'd ever produced.

They were almost to the bottling facility. He could hear the clink of glass, the whir of the machines. The smell of bourbon whisky permeated the air. Something deep inside him shifted. It said, *I love this. I love being here. With her.*

Ross stopped. Frowned. Holly moved on, oblivious, phone to her ear as she talked to a supplier about something. She disappeared into the bottling area. He remained where he was, smelling the old wood of the building, the charred oak of the barrels, the bourbon and mash. The glasses clinked, the machines whirred, and the building felt alive somehow.

His equilibrium was shifting, like a river finding new channels.

He shook his head. What the hell? He was a Blackthorne, but he was a Blackthorne who didn't feel the whisky moving in his blood. It wasn't his thing.

And yet it called to him. Somehow. Some way. The whisky called.

And not just the whisky. The Kentucky bluegrass. The people and customs. The land. The distillery itself with its picturesque setting—the creek and pond, the old oak trees that stood tall, the house on the hill. The buildings that bore his family name but had once bore hers.

Holly's face appeared in the glass door to the bottling room. She came out again, walking toward him, her red hair flowing down over her shoulders, her skin so creamy white and perfect. She wore a dress today because they'd had a meeting with distributors. It was pale blue and it wrapped around her like a glove, showcasing her gorgeous body. She'd worn heels earlier but of course she'd put on a pair of Converse once the distributors were gone.

The top three-quarters of her reminded him of women in the racing world—polished, perfect, assets on display. But her feet? That was pure Holly Brooks.

His heart thumped hard. Feelings whirled in his brain, feelings he'd never had before. What the hell was wrong with him?

"Hey? Everything okay?" she asked, looking worried as she approached.

He wanted to grab her. Kiss her. Push her back against the wall and unzip that dress. He already knew it had a side zipper. He'd spent almost twenty minutes in a meeting this morning staring at it and thinking about the moment he got to pull it down. Then he'd push the edges open and feast his eyes and mouth on her gorgeous form.

But he couldn't do that. Not here in the middle of the distillery. There were employees, tourists, and probably even a few cameras trained on them.

"Yeah, it's fine. I was thinking."

Her eyes searched his. Concerned. He loved that she cared about him. He cared about her too.

"Do you need to take a break?"

"What I need," he said, low enough that only she could hear, "is to peel that dress off you."

She flushed pink. He loved it when she did that. "Why do you think I'm still wearing it instead of changing into something else? As soon as we walk through the door tonight, I'm expecting you to do just that."

He grinned at her. "Oh baby, I'm going to. Maybe even with my teeth."

She looked shocked. Then she laughed. "I'm counting on it, Ross. Now come on, bottling waits for no one."

"Yes, ma'am," he said.

But as he followed her through the doors, he knew something was changing. He just didn't know what. Or if he was fully ready to accept it.

Chapter 16

They went to Muriel's again, partly because of the food and partly because of the high-backed booths, which meant Ross could hide just a little bit. Glenda served them, chatty as usual. Ross flirted with her and she blushed and playfully smacked him on the shoulder as she poured more sweet tea into his glass.

Billy Truesville was bussing tables tonight. When he got to a table nearby, Holly could tell that he recognized Ross from the last time. He didn't say anything though. Probably too shy to do so.

"Hey, Billy," Ross said, and Billy looked up with wide eyes. Then he smiled so broadly that Holly's heart ached for him. He'd thought Ross wouldn't remember him. It was written clear as day on the kid's face, and now that Ross had, Billy lit up from the inside.

"Hey, Ross. I didn't see your car out there. Didn't know you were here."

"You didn't see the Super Snake?"

Billy nodded. "Oh yes, I saw that. Cool truck. Is that yours too?"

"Sure is. You want to see it?"

Billy clutched the tub of dishes he was holding. "I'd love to. But I don't get a break for another hour."

"That's okay," Ross said. "We just got here a few minutes ago. I'm sure we'll still be enjoying dinner."

"Awesome. Thank you. I better get back to work."

"Swing by when you're on break," Ross told him.

"I will. Thanks!" Billy practically floated to the next table.

Holly's heart was still aching. But not for Billy. For the man in front of her who was so damned thoughtful of others. Ross didn't have to pay attention to a teenager whose dad was in prison and who worked to help his mom make ends meet. But he did. Because he was a good guy. An amazing guy.

The kind of guy a woman could love.

Holly's stomach fluttered. Her heart started to hammer. If she'd been standing, she'd have had to sit down again.

No way.

There was no way she was in love with Ross Black-thorne. It was impossible. Not to mention it was the dumbest thing she could possibly do. Fall for a guy because he was nice and sweet and great in bed? Really?

Yes, her heart whispered.

That's exactly how you fell for someone. They made you happy and they were somehow the best person you knew. Her heart knew it even while her brain continued to argue in circles.

Not possible, too soon, it's just a phase, you'll come to your senses…

But no, it was the truth. She felt the weight of it in her soul.

Holly felt like someone had sucked all the oxygen from

the room. She sat there blinking, not really hearing anything, waiting for the world to catch up.

Oh God, she was in so much trouble here.

"You look pale," Ross said, frowning. "You okay?"

Her stomach was a knot of tension. "I, uh, no. I feel a little light-headed."

His expression instantly morphed to one of extreme concern. "Do we need to go? Should you lie down? Can I get anything for you?"

She waved him off with a weak laugh. *Breathe, dammit.* "No, it's okay. I'm probably just hungry. It's been hours since lunch."

Glenda chose that moment to return with a basket of hush puppies. Holly seized on one, not quite certain she could stomach it but determined to try anyway. They had to hang around so Billy could see the truck. And there was nothing wrong with her other than she'd just realized she was in love with a man who not only had power over her job (for now), but also wasn't likely to stay at the distillery beyond the moment his father gave him the okay to return to racing.

Damned if you do, damned if you don't.

They started talking about things that had happened at the distillery that day. She seized on the conversation, grateful because it was about work and she could focus on work instead of these crazy feelings swirling inside her. Ross was talking about the bottling and ideas for how to package any new flavored bourbons they might produce when Holly tilted her head to look at him.

"What?" he asked.

"Why Ross Blackthorne, I do believe you're displaying an *interest* in the distillery. How is this possible?"

He laughed. "I'm as shocked as you are. But things are starting to make sense to me. I mean I don't want to sit in an office and pretend I know what I'm doing, but I kinda get why people get addicted to crafting fine whisky. Not everybody can do it, can they?"

She shook her head and smiled. "No, they can't. And I think I understand why people like fast cars."

"Not just fast ones. Unique ones."

"Those too. I like the older one you have. The red Italian one. What was it?"

"I've got a few, but I think you mean the Pantera."

"Yes. The lines are so sleek. But I also like the older Corvette too."

"It's a classic. Same body style as the movie *Corvette Summer*."

"I never saw that."

"It's an old movie. The guy from *Star Wars* was in it. Luke Skywalker."

Glenda bustled over then with their food, interrupting the conversation. "Here you go. Two catfish specials. Tartar sauce, green beans, and fries." She straightened again. "Ross, thank you for being so nice to Billy. He's just bouncing around back there. Harry says he can take his break whenever y'all are ready. That way you don't have to wait around."

"He's a nice kid and he likes cars. It's the least I can do. Thank Harry for me, please."

"I will. Billy hasn't stopped talking about that fancy car of yours since you were in here before. His dad had an old Camaro they were going to fix up together, but that man was as useless as tits on a bull. He never intended to fix a thing. Damned car just sits in the yard, rusting away."

Somebody at another table waved. "Gotta go, sugar," she said to Ross, giving him a pat on the arm as she did so.

Ross was staring speculatively at his plate.

"What is it, Ross?"

"I need to open that garage, don't I? Start fixing up cars for people who need them. Billy's almost sixteen. He'll need a car to get around."

Holly swallowed the lump in her throat. "It's your call, but it sounds like something that would be great."

"There's a lot of work to do—finding a location, building the facility, hiring the mechanics and staff. And I need to get the plans in place before I return to racing. Because once that happens, I won't have time."

Holly's chest tightened. She picked up a fry and ate it. It tasted like dust. Of course he still wanted to return to racing. Expected to return.

For him, nothing had changed. For her, she'd just discovered the most momentous thing to ever happen to her. Between one breath and the next, her life had changed irrevocably.

She was in love.

And he was trying to figure out how to build a garage without cutting into his racing schedule. It wasn't his fault she was gutted by his casual announcement. It was hers.

And she couldn't let him know it.

"You're rich," she said lightly. "You can hire people to do everything for you. And you can talk to people via Skype or Face Time when you're on the road. This isn't really all that hard, Ross."

He was still frowning. "No," he finally said. "Maybe it's not."

She took a bite of catfish. It was flaky and crispy and she didn't taste a thing. "I have no doubt you'll get it done. You can start now while you know you're working at the distillery for the foreseeable future. Then when you go out on the road again, the ball will already be rolling."

"You're right. The sooner I get started, the better."

"Absolutely," she said, her throat closing up.

He grinned. "Thanks, Holly. If you hadn't picked Muriel's the first time we went to dinner, I'd have never met Billy or realized how much impact I can have right now instead of someday."

"You're going to do terrific things, Ross. I know you will."

He reached over and squeezed her hand. "Thanks to you."

"No, it's all you. You're a great guy."

He arched an eyebrow. "That's something I'd have never thought you'd say two weeks ago."

Holly's smile felt brittle. Probably was brittle since she felt like her heart was breaking inside. "There are a lot of things I never thought I'd say or do two weeks ago. But I'm glad I did."

No matter how much they ended up hurting when this was over.

ROSS COULDN'T SLEEP. Beside him, Holly lay completely still, softly breathing.

After they'd eaten at Muriel's, they'd returned to her house and made fast, furious love just inside the door, unable to make it to the bed for the first round.

They'd made it there for the second. Holly had come apart so easily, so beautifully, beneath his touch. But something had felt off. There was a distance between them tonight, a distance he didn't recall feeling before.

It had to be what he'd said about returning to racing. He'd said it because he'd always assumed his dad would relent and he'd be back with the team. It'd been his light in the darkness and the ultimate goal he'd kept his sights on.

But saying it hadn't felt the way it should. It hadn't made him happy.

Holly made him happy.

He was at a crossroads. He knew it in his bones. He loved driving, loved the speed and danger of the race. But he also wanted Holly beside him. Why couldn't he have both?

It shouldn't be that difficult, not really. He was still based in Kentucky. He could sell the house, buy something in Lexington to be closer to her. The only thing that would change is that he wouldn't be at the distillery anymore. She'd have her domain back, which he thought would make her happy.

And yet the idea of not being at the distillery with Holly—not seeing her smile that was only for him, not watching her serious expression as she tested the mash or tasted the first drops of whisky from an aged barrel, not seeing her red hair gleaming like copper as she strode down the aisle of a barrelhouse when the sun was setting— was painful in a way that surprised him.

He liked being at Blackthorne Kentucky with Holly. He liked how important it was to her, how hard she worked, and how she never forgot her own family's history or traditions when it came to the whisky.

And it wasn't just Holly. He liked Evan Brooks and the whole team. They were filled with pride in their jobs, and they contributed a great deal to the Blackthorne bottom line. Yes, his father had bought Brooks Creek and built bigger and better facilities.

But without these workers who lived and breathed bourbon whisky, Blackthorne would not thrive here. The Blackthornes weren't from here, and that kind of tradition meant a lot in the South. Especially in Bourbon County where there was pride for a whisky that went back centuries and was named for this patch of land in Kentucky.

Other distilleries made bourbon-style. They did not make bourbon.

Ross lay there for a long time, thinking. No matter how many angles he considered it from, no matter how often he asked himself *what if,* there was only one answer he could come up with.

Ultimately, he knew what he had to do. He only hoped it was right—and that Holly would forgive him.

Chapter 17

The Kentucky Speedway was jammed with people who happily shouted and drank beer and cheered on the drivers as they sped around the oval track. It was a seething mass of humanity who'd all come out for a sport that was loud and smelly and dirty.

And exciting as heck. Couldn't forget that part, because it was much more exciting in person than it had been on television.

Holly had toured the pit with Ross, met his crew, his driver, and been overwhelmed with the noises and smells. Rubber was the predominant smell once the cars began their laps. Gas was big on the list too. And there was road grit that got into your nose and onto your skin if you hung around out there for very long during the race.

They had not, thankfully. Holly thought Ross wanted to, and she'd been willing if it's what he wanted, but he'd said goodbye to everyone, taken her hand, and led her to an air-conditioned suite where finely dressed people mingled, drank, and watched the race from on high. And where they did not have to wear ear protection.

"Wow, this view," Holly said as they walked inside.

"It's great, right?"

"Sure is."

They didn't get to say much more because Ross was suddenly mobbed by people who came over to talk to him.

Holly took one look at the women—most of them dressed to the nines—and felt a little out of place. She'd worn a cotton sundress and kitten heels and Ross had told her she looked amazing when she'd emerged from getting dressed this morning at his house.

She'd stayed overnight with him because his house was closer to the track. It'd only been a couple of days since she'd realized she was in love with him and every day was more poignant and worrying than the last. She thought, for her heart's sake, that maybe she should pull back, put some distance between them.

But she couldn't do it. She wanted to be with him because she loved the way she felt when they were together. They way he worshipped her body so tenderly and did everything he could to make her happy.

Maybe that was just Ross when he was with someone, or maybe it was something more. She wanted it to be more, but she knew she couldn't fool herself that it was. That would not be healthy.

She'd decided to enjoy this weekend, because he'd asked her to, but she was always conscious of a ticking doomsday clock somewhere in her head. Counting down the minutes until he left the distillery and returned to the track.

Ross had been holding her hand when they walked into the suite, but he'd let go to shake hands and hug people. Holly stayed beside him, and he introduced her to everyone.

After a few minutes, she touched his elbow. He gazed down at her, smiling, the happiness apparent on his face.

He loved being here. With these people. This was his world. She felt out of place in it, but he was a natural. Her heart throbbed.

"I'm going to freshen up," she said quietly.

He bent and kissed her on the cheek in front of everyone. She tucked a lock of hair that had escaped her hair clip behind her ear, knowing she was blushing but unable to stop it. "Do you know where it is?" he asked softly, for her ears only.

"Yes. Have fun, Ross. I'll be back."

"Okay, honey."

Holly turned and headed for the lounge she'd seen. She pushed into the ladies' room, intending to use the facilities and freshen her makeup. She was underdressed and under-made up when compared to many of the women in the suite. There was a lounge with chairs and fluffy sofas, mirrors and soft lighting before she reached a louvered door that led to the restroom itself.

Holly took care of business, then washed her hands and pulled her lipstick out of her purse. She was applying the lipstick when she heard voices from the lounge. They did not enter the restroom but seemed to be staying in the seating area.

"Did you see that girl with Ross Blackthorne?" one of them said.

Another voice, higher pitched, trilled, "Where did he find her? A farm?"

"That outfit. It's so sweet, right? Her hair piled on top of her head with a clip. So tacky. And those heels. He cannot seriously be interested in that woman. She's so plain next to him."

"Well," the higher-pitched voice said, "she's definitely not right for him."

"Definitely not."

"She won't last. They never do."

The other woman laughed. "Once he's back on the circuit, Miss Kentucky Farm Girl will be history."

"She'll probably throw herself down a well or something. Poor thing."

They laughed together like a pair of cackling witches. Holly seethed. She didn't know who they were. They could be any of the ladies who'd been circling around out there.

How would she go back into the suite now? Heck, how could she escape the restroom if they stayed in the lounge? Ross could be wondering where she was, and she was trapped by a pair of bitches baying at the base of the tree.

Holly suppressed a laugh at that image. Yeah, she was pissed all right. And hurt, because it never felt good to overhear people making fun of you. But one thing she wasn't was a victim.

Screw them.

Holly drew herself up. Sucked in a couple of breaths. Turned to the mirror and unclipped her hair from the top of her head. She'd put it up because of the heat, but she knew it was gorgeous when she let it down. She shook it out, finger-combed it into fluffy waves.

Then she pushed the door to the lounge and walked boldly into it, kitten heels, sundress and all. "Ladies," she said as she sailed by. She stopped at the door and turned to look at them. The woman with the higher voice had the grace to look uncomfortable. The other was staring with dislike.

They were wearing skintight dresses that showed their perfect figures, with heels that were at least five inches high, and their hair was artfully curled and fluffed around their faces. Their makeup was perfection. They were both lovely—except for where it counted.

"I'm afraid we have city water on the farm now," Holly said. "No wells to throw myself down. Y'all have a blessed day."

Holly was perspiring as she left the ladies' lounge. Yes, it was satisfactory to tell those bitches off. But it only hammered home the true point of the day.

She did not belong in this world. Not at all.

ERIC VICKER PULLED off a stunning upset, passing the lead car and taking the checkered flag. Ross jumped out of his seat, shouting. The suite was boiling with tension that erupted when the Blackthorne car crossed the finish in first place.

Hell, some of them wouldn't be happy about that. But some of them would. And Ross was happiest of all. The win was just icing on the cake of everything else that had happened today.

It was a good damned day.

He turned to his favorite person in the whole room. She was beside him, cheering with him. He grabbed her in his arms and kissed her. He didn't care who saw.

"Oh Ross," she said when he let her up for air. "I know you wanted to be the one driving, but I'm so happy your team won."

"I am too, Holly."

She searched his gaze. "Are you really?"

"Yes." He squeezed her softly. "I'm here with you, not out there in a hot car on a hot track with all the noise and vibration. I kinda like it from this viewpoint."

He'd thought he'd feel on edge being at the track today.

Thought he'd ache to be behind the wheel. But the truth was he'd enjoyed watching Eric drive. He could have sat in the pit stand where the nerve center of the team was, but Holly wouldn't have been comfortable there. It didn't matter anyway because he was in constant communication with his crew while sitting here like a sponsor and watching the race unfold.

"Let's go congratulate them."

She smiled. "That sounds like a plan. But no spraying me with champagne, okay?"

He laughed. "Nobody's spraying you with champagne. Except maybe me. At home. When you're naked."

She blushed. "Ross."

"I'll let you spray me too."

Her lashed dipped. "We'll see."

They headed for victory lane where his team was starting to celebrate like crazy. Eric had done the requisite donuts in the infield and now the car was parked in front of the stand.

Ross got lots of congratulations on the way there, and some commiserations that he hadn't been the one driving. Ross accepted it all, waved off the gloaters—because there were always some—and kept on going.

Martin Temple was grinning ear to ear. "Ross, geez, did you see that?"

"Sure did. The car performed beautifully. You've made an amazing machine, Martin."

"No blown engines today."

"Thank God," Ross said.

Martin laughed. "Oh, it'll happen again. You know it will."

"Yep. Always does."

Eric was busy pumping his fists in victory. When he saw

Ross, he came running over and threw his arms around Ross's shoulders, clapping him on the back.

"Congrats, buddy," Ross said. "Awesome driving today."

"Thank you, Ross. Thanks so much for giving me the opportunity."

"You earned it, man. Celebrate."

"Yes, sir!" Eric headed for the car and jumped up on the hood as the crowd roared.

Reporters were everywhere and several of them headed for Ross when they realized he was there. Within seconds, he had microphones shoved in his face. He held Holly's hand tightly so she wouldn't get separated from him.

She stuck by his side, and he was grateful for it. He didn't want to do this without her.

"Ross, how did it feel to watch the Blackthorne car out there without you today?"

"Ross, why aren't you driving?"

"Ross, when are you returning to the track?"

"Ross, is it true you're leaving Blackthorne Racing?"

That last question caught his attention for sure. There was always speculation in stock racing's circles, but this was so specific that he knew someone had been talking somewhere.

He pushed his way to that microphone. The other reporters seemed to shrink a little bit in order to give space for the one who'd asked the question.

"Well, Dirk," he drawled. "I haven't actually discussed this with my team yet, so you're getting an exclusive here. I'm not leaving the team—for now."

"For now? What's that mean?"

He could feel the tension in Holly's body. He gave her hand a reassuring squeeze. "It means I've been on the phone with corporate and I've agreed to stick around for as long as they need me to represent the brand."

Holly's chest rose and fell a little faster beside him. He could see it out of the corner of his eye. Her hand tightened on his. He didn't know if she knew it or not.

"But I will not be driving. I'm retiring from the circuit, effective immediately."

The news rippled through the reporters like a flash fire. Holly had gone still. He looked down at her. Her eyes were wide as she stared up at him. He didn't know what was going on behind those eyes. How she was feeling, what she was thinking.

Her jaw fell open.

"Say something," he said softly.

Holly burst into tears.

Chapter 18

Oh God, she was a total idiot. She'd just proven herself to be the unsophisticated farm girl those women said she was. She'd burst into tears during Ross's interview.

And she couldn't seem to stop.

He shouldered the reporters aside, his arm protectively around her as he steered her away from the crowd. She didn't know where they were going, but somehow he found a place out of the way. It was still noisy with celebration, and people still walked by, but they were about as alone as they could be. Which wasn't a whole lot.

"I'm sorry," she said, wiping her eyes. "That was stupid of me."

His hands were on her shoulders. "Look at me, Holly."

She managed it, her chin quivering, her eyes blurrier then she'd like. "Sorry."

He wiped away her tears with his shirtsleeve. "It's okay. Maybe I should say I'm sorry."

She sniffled. "Why?"

"For not warning you. I know you don't necessarily

want me at the distillery, but I thought maybe I could be a veep at large or something."

Holly was having trouble processing everything he'd just said. "It's not about you being at the distillery."

"It's not?"

Stupid man.

"No." Her throat was tight. "If you race, then you travel. There'd be no time for… this. Us."

Her heart thrummed to say that word. Us. What if he didn't think there was an us? He might have retired from racing for any number of reasons that had nothing to do with her.

He smiled, his grin broad and maybe even a little smug. "You want me to stay?"

"I'm getting used to having you around. You might even be a good distiller someday."

He laughed. "That's high praise coming from you."

"Damn right." She sniffled. "I can't believe I cried in front of all those people. And now those women are going to think they were right about me."

He frowned. "What women?"

"The ones who said I was a farm girl and you could do better."

His nostrils flared, his mouth flattening. "Tell me who they are."

"No. It's not important. I took care of it."

His eyebrows rose. Then he laughed. "I bet you did."

She told him what she'd said and he laughed harder. "Okay, you win. Nobody puts my Holly down and gets away with it."

His Holly. She liked that. But she still didn't know what any of this meant. If it had a thing to do with her or if it was just a decision handed down from his father.

"Did you really retire from racing?"

He nodded. "Yes."

"Of your own free will?"

"Yes."

"Why?"

He put his hands on her hips, dragged her toward him. "For this. Us. *You.*"

Holly gulped. "But why?"

"Because I'm in love with you."

All the oxygen seemed to be sucked from the air around her. Holly stared up at him, gaping like a fish. Hope flooded her. But of course doubt was there, because she was who she was and things never seemed to turn out the way she wanted them to.

"But how do you know? We just met."

"Trust me when I tell you I know. This has never happened to me before. Never. I know what I'm feeling. It's love. For you. Because I want you to be happy. You're my first thought in the morning and my last at night. You're the person I want to be with, the one whose smile lights up the sky. You're it for me, Holly Brooks. I saw you walking toward me that first day at the distillery, with your clipboard and your scowl, and I haven't thought of anyone else since."

She was shaking. Literally shaking. "You're a glutton for punishment then."

He laughed. "No, I'm crazy in love with you. And I want to stay in Kentucky. Where you are."

She was going to cry again.

Still.

Whatever.

"I don't want you giving up your dreams for me."

"I'm not. In fact, you're the reason I'm going for my dreams. I talked to my father yesterday and told him I'm going out on my own. Opening Ross Blackthorne Motorsports. I'll use my own money, and I've already lined up sponsors. I don't need to win the Cup for that. And I'm building those garages, too. Billy's car will be first—but for him I'm doing a complete overhaul. That sucker is going to shine—but reasonably because I don't want anyone trying to steal it from him."

She loved this man. So much. "And Blackthorne Racing?"

"I'm staying on as executive director. I told my dad I was leaving, but he asked me to stay in an advisory role. I can do that. I expect he'll shift the racing division to my company when it's time anyway. That'll be a few years, probably. But it doesn't matter if he does or not. RB Motorsports will be mine, and nobody gets to tell me who to hire or what to do anymore."

"Does this mean you're leaving the distillery?"

"Do you want me to?"

She traced a heart on his shirt. Over and over again. "No, I don't. Unless you don't want to be there. That's different."

"I thought I'd work there part time, learn the business from top to bottom, if that's okay with you. The rest of the time I'll run my motorsport company and the garages. I'm going to build as close to the distillery as I can."

"You know what, Ross?"

"What?"

"All I want is for you to be happy. Because you're it for me too. I love you. You're the best man I know, and I'm so lucky that you're mine."

He picked her up and she squealed as he twirled her around. Then he slid her down his body and kissed her so thoroughly she forgot where they were or the fact they were far from alone. It took distant cheering to realize they weren't. They broke apart, but the cheering continued. It was for Eric and the Blackthorne crew, not for them.

Ross grinned. Holly grinned too. "Should we go back out there?" he asked. "Tell the world you're my girl and we're moving in together?"

She blinked. And then she laughed. "I guess we are, aren't we? But where?"

"We'll shop for a house together. Something that feels like a home."

"With a fifty-car garage."

He snorted. "Maybe not that many."

"Are you kidding me? You're like some of these women with their shoe closets, I swear."

He laughed as he took her hand and they strolled back out to victory lane. Confetti and champagne flowed freely and the Blackthorne crew looked tired and happy. Eric Vicker was hoisting his trophy and grinning ear to ear. A crew of gorgeous models flanked him.

"Will you miss that?" Holly asked Ross as they watched.

"Not in the least. I'd miss this a lot more." He leaned down and kissed her, and Holly knew without a doubt he meant it.

There was love in that kiss. Promise. A future.

ROSS WALKED into the Blackthorne Distillery on Monday and encountered a frowning Evan Brooks.

"Ross. Can you kindly tell me what your intentions are toward my niece?"

The footage from the race had been played everywhere, apparently. The moment he'd announced his retirement, Holly bursting into tears—and them off in a space between trailers talking, getting closer, and then kissing. It was an invasion of their privacy, but there was nothing to be done for it now.

"Yes, sir. I intend to marry her, though we're planning to move in together first."

He knew that didn't sound very good, but he knew Holly well enough to know that she'd want some time together before they walked down the aisle. But they would walk down the aisle. He was certain of that.

"Do you love her?"

"I do."

"How can you be certain?"

Was it a family trait or what? "Because her smile lights the sky and I can't live without her."

Evan frowned a bit harder. Then he laughed and held out a hand. "Welcome to the family, Ross."

"It's an honor, Mr. Brooks."

"Holly's going to be the master distiller here when I retire. You realize that, right?"

"Of course I do."

Evan nodded. "Good man. Holly's a good kid. She deserves the best you can give her. One hundred percent."

"It's my intention to give it to her. Every day."

Holly emerged from a hallway and stopped when she saw them. She smiled at Ross, that smile that made his world bright. "Is everything okay?" she asked.

"It is," Evan said. "Just having a talk with Ross."

Holly came over and stood beside him. "Now Uncle Evan—"

"Calm down, girl. It's all good." He walked away, grumbling, and Holly turned to Ross.

"Is it?"

"Yes. Your uncle loves you. He wants to make sure I do too."

She kissed him, a quick peck on the lips. They definitely weren't hiding anything anymore, but they weren't going to engage in a lot of PDA either. "I know you do."

They started to walk toward their offices. "I just got the oddest call," she said.

"Oh yeah?"

"I mean it was a good call, but still."

"What was it?"

"Emily's doctor. He said she's been put in for an experimental therapy program—and there are no out-of-pocket expenses whatsoever."

Ross tried to keep a straight face when she turned to look at him. He failed. Her eyes narrowed as she stared. They'd stopped outside her office door.

"Did you have anything to do with that?" she asked.

"Depends on if you're going to be mad or not."

Her eyes widened. "Mad? Oh Ross, how could I be mad?" She started to sniffle and he produced a tissue from his pocket. He'd prepared.

"I didn't tell you because I didn't know if there were any programs or not. He wouldn't tell me anything because I'm not related to your sister. But I gave him a blank check to do what he needs. You and your family will have to approve anything, of course. But I thought if there was a chance…"

Holly was dabbing her eyes like crazy. "You didn't have to do it. I love you no matter what—but I love that you did this for her. Dr. Brown said it may not work and not to get my hopes up. But it's a start."

He opened her office door and pushed her inside, barely getting it closed before she threw her arms around him and kissed him. He held her tightly against his body, loving the way this woman felt in his arms.

Perfect. So perfect.

"If you don't stop, I'm going to push all that paper off your desk and use it in ways it was never meant to be used," he told her when they came up for air.

She giggled. "I might like that. But maybe not first thing on a Monday when everybody just found out we're dating."

His body throbbed. "Some night when everyone's gone home then."

"Oh yes. Mmm, I'm imagining it now."

"Don't put that in my head, Holly. I'll be stuck in here for hours because I won't be able to walk around without an erection."

She sighed and put her arms around his torso, hugging him close. He stroked his hand down her back, willing himself to cool off.

"I love you," she said.

"I love you too."

He leaned against the door, Holly in his arms, and knew that everything was exactly as it was meant to be. He was a Blackthorne, filled with a daredevil spirit and a drive to succeed, but also bred to make fine whisky.

He was opening up his own motorsport company. Building his garages. Consulting for the racing division. But mostly, he was loving this woman in his arms. Because she made everything possible.

The mighty Ross Blackthorne had fallen.

And he was enjoying every minute of it… for the rest of his life.

Author's Note

Astute fans of NASCAR might notice some mistakes. I tried very hard not to make them, but the sport is complicated and I'm not perfect. For simplicity's sake, I didn't go into the different series or how Ross got into Monster Energy (the biggie). I imagine he came up through the ranks like most. I tried not to go into details, mostly because a casual reader likely wouldn't be too interested, but I wanted what I included to be as accurate as I could make it.

If it's not, I apologize.

I am not personally a gear head like Ross is, but I do love cars. Especially fast ones. I can appreciate an exotic sports car even if I can't afford one. I've sat in a Ferrari and a Lamborghini. Not Ross's Ferrari, though. That is a rare and expensive beast.

If you don't know much about NASCAR and want to know more, just start Googling. It's quite fascinating. And if you ever get to go to a race, trust me, it's as loud, gritty, and exciting as I described in the book. I discovered that at Talladega one October....

Also by Lynn Raye Harris

The HOT SEAL Team Books

Book 1: HOT SEAL - Dane & Ivy

Book 2: HOT SEAL Lover - Remy & Christina

Book 3: HOT SEAL Rescue - Cody & Miranda

Book 4: HOT SEAL BRIDE - Cash & Ella

Book 5: HOT SEAL REDEMPTION - Alex & Bailey

Book 6: HOT SEAL TARGET - Blade & Quinn

Book 7: HOT SEAL HERO - Dirty & Chloe

The Hostile Operations Team Books

Book 0: RECKLESS HEAT

Book 1: HOT PURSUIT - Matt & Evie

Book 2: HOT MESS - Sam & Georgie

Book 3: HOT PACKAGE - Billy & Olivia

Book 4: DANGEROUSLY HOT - Kev & Lucky

Book 5: HOT SHOT - Jack & Gina

Book 6: HOT REBEL - Nick & Victoria

Book 7: HOT ICE - Garrett & Grace

Book 8: HOT & BOTHERED - Ryan & Emily

Book 9: HOT PROTECTOR - Chase & Sophie

Book 10: HOT ADDICTION - Dex & Annabelle

Book 11: HOT VALOR - Mendez & Kat

Book 12: HOT ANGEL - Cade & Brooke

Book 13: HOT SECRETS - Sky & Bliss

Book 14: HOT JUSTICE ~ Wolf & Haylee

The HOT Novella in Liliana Hart's MacKenzie Family Series

HOT WITNESS - Jake & Eva

7 Brides for 7 Brothers

MAX (Book 5) - Max & Ellie

7 Brides for 7 Soldiers

WYATT (Book 4) - Wyatt & Paige

About the Author

Lynn Raye Harris is the *New York Times* and *USA Today* bestselling author of the HOSTILE OPERATIONS TEAM SERIES of military romances as well as 20 books for Harlequin Presents. A former finalist for the Romance Writers of America's Golden Heart Award and the National Readers Choice Award, Lynn lives in Alabama with her handsome former-military husband, two crazy cats, and one spoiled American Saddlebred horse. Lynn's books have been called "exceptional and emotional," "intense," and "sizzling." Lynn's books have sold over 3 million copies worldwide.

To connect with Lynn online:
www.LynnRayeHarris.com
Lynn@LynnRayeHarris.com

Made in the USA
Coppell, TX
01 July 2021